soldier
on

sydney logan

dedication

For my friend, Denise,
who told me I should write a book about it.

Matthew 5:4

chapter one

Stephanie

I'm going to kill Tessa for dragging me here.

What started out as just a few friends quickly turned into a rowdy frat house mixer on New Year's Eve. Hip-hop music blares, and the thick, smoky haze makes me sick to my stomach. The co-eds who can still stand are dancing in the middle of the living room. Some have found secluded areas of the house to make out, while others play video games in the den.

I get it. This is all supposedly part of the college experience. But keg parties are the one aspect of campus life I despise, and I guarantee I'm the only one drinking soda instead of beer. I've always hated the smell, and I definitely hate the taste. Besides, I see nothing fun about puking in the bushes or hooking up with random guys. I'm not a prude, but I can recognize a stupidly dangerous situation when I see one, and this party is a recipe for disaster.

I check my watch and notice it's close to midnight, so I send a quick text to Tessa, my best friend and roommate, to see if she needs a ride back to the apartment. Knowing Tessa and her boyfriend, Xavier, they are probably one of the couples in the upstairs bedrooms. If that's the case, my presence is no longer required. I *hope* that's the case.

While waiting for her reply, a guy dressed as Luke Skywalker walks up to me.

If he asks me to touch his lightsaber, I'm out of here.

"Can I get you a drink?"

His breath reeks of alcohol, and my stomach twists. I lift the red plastic cup that hasn't left my hand all night.

"No, thanks. I'm good."

His gaze sweeps over my costume. "Nice dress."

"Thanks."

"Disney, right? That girl who likes to read."

"Right."

Dressing up as Belle from *Beauty and the Beast* had seemed like a good idea at the time. The party's theme was "Movie Night," and Tessa had found this short and sexy version of Belle's yellow dress in a vintage costume store in town.

Belle had never shown this much leg. Or cleavage.

The guy steps closer. "So, Belle, wanna dance?"

"My name's Stephanie."

"Okay . . . Stephanie. Wanna dance?"

"No, thanks."

"Wanna touch my lightsaber?"

Totally called it.

"No, but I'll be happy to break it."

The guy's face pales before he quickly slinks back into the shadows.

With a disgusted sigh, I toss my cup into a nearby, overflowing trash can before maneuvering my way through the dancers and up the stairs in search of my best friend. Bravely, I try a few of the rooms, but all are locked except for a set of open double doors at the end of the hallway.

Curious, I step inside, and I'm instantly mesmerized.

Frat houses have libraries?

This one does, complete with ceiling-high bookshelves. Laptops line one wall, and a giant multimedia screen is attached to another. While all of it is impressive, nothing excites my book-loving heart more than to see the library ladder.

Secretly, I've always wanted to climb one—the tall ladders that roll from one end of the shelves to the other. Ironically enough, library ladders always remind me of *Beauty and the Beast*. Or the love scene in *Atonement*.

One of those movies is G-rated. The other most definitely is not.

Suddenly nervous, I look over my shoulder before making my decision.

YOLO. Carpe Diem. Whatever.

Slipping off my shoes, I reach for the ladder and slowly begin to climb. Sadly, this is the most adventurous thing I've done in a long time, and I can't stop smiling. I've made it to the fifth rung when I hear someone clear his throat.

Crap. Please don't be Luke Skywalker.

I hold on tightly and manage to turn myself around without falling off. When I'm sure I'm steady, I turn and find myself looking into the eyes of a soldier. Possibly Army. Maybe Marine.

Not that it matters. I accepted long ago that my hatred for anything military related is a little unhealthy, but when the service strips a girl of the privilege of knowing her father, it sometimes makes a person bitter.

I am the epitome of bitter.

This particular solider is smiling at me, and I can't lie, the smile is kind of beautiful. Despite that, my first instinct is to roll my eyes at his outfit. But then, I remember this is a costume party, and he probably just needed a quick and totally uncreative disguise.

"I don't think this room is open to visitors," he says, his tone soft and deep.

I wonder if that's his natural speaking voice or if he's just playing his role as a badass. The guy certainly *looks* like a soldier, dressed in his head-to-toe camouflage and smeared-on face paint.

"It was actually the only room that wasn't locked, which is kind of stupid if you ask me. This is the one room in the house you guys shouldn't want trashed. Drunken idiots could really do some damage in here."

He grins, and my breath catches in my throat as he steps closer. I tighten my hold on the ladder, because a smile that makes a girl's heart race isn't the best thing when she's trying to maintain her balance.

"I noticed you downstairs."

Embarrassed, I glance down at my ridiculous dress. "I'm a little hard to miss in canary yellow. I'm going to kill Tessa—"

"That's not why I noticed you."

He's closer now, with one hand pressed against the shelf behind me. He's tall, but thanks to the ladder, we're practically nose-to-nose. Normally, I would be frightened of a complete stranger invading my space, but honestly, this is the most relaxed I've felt all night. With his athletic build, there's no doubt he could hurt me if he wanted, but I'm not afraid. For one thing, his breath doesn't stink and his speech isn't slurred. For another, he's gazing at me with a pair of big brown eyes that make my stomach do this weird somersault-thing, and my stomach hasn't done somersaults in a very long time.

Before I can ask why he noticed me, shouts erupt from downstairs.

"Ten, nine, eight . . ."

"Do you have someone to kiss at midnight?" he asks.

I simply shake my head. He steps closer, pinning me between his body and the bookshelf.

"You do now."

Horns blare below, but I barely notice because in the next second, his mouth covers mine. His lips are featherlight and sweet, causing warmth to spread through my veins and settle in my heart. I sigh, causing my lips to part slightly, allowing him to deepen the kiss. One of his hands stroke my cheek as he leans in, pressing his body tighter against mine. His quiet groan vibrates through me, and I'm ready to let go of the ladder and wrap my arms around him when he suddenly pulls away.

"Wow," he whispers.

I'll say.

I open my eyes, and all I can see is his smile.

"Happy New Year," he says.

Then he's gone, sprinting from the room before I can even formulate a coherent response.

In a daze, I carefully climb down the ladder and step into my shoes. While the celebration roars below my feet, I flip off the lights and close the door before heading downstairs.

"There you are!" Tessa says, grabbing my arm as I reach the landing. "I've been looking all over the place for you since I got your text. I am *so* ready to go. Xavier wants to stay and play video games, but I'm . . . Steph? Are you okay?"

"I'm fine."

She squints and examines my face. "Have you been drinking? You never drink."

"No, I haven't been drinking."

"Are you sure? Because you look a little drunk."

Shaking my head, I snap out of my daze and pull her toward the door. It's only when we're outside in the frigid air do I manage to come to my senses. I spin toward my best friend, whose eyes grow wide as I tell her about my New Year's kiss.

"Steph, that's amazing! What's his name?"

The simple question kills my momentary excitement and knocks me right out of my dazed state.

I just had the most perfect kiss of my life, and I don't even know his name.

"Is that you, Steph?"

"It's me."

I let the door slam behind me and drop my backpack on the floor. The apartment smells delicious, but right now, all I want is the couch. The first day of classes seriously kicked my ass.

Tessa runs out of the kitchen, wiping her hands on the apron tied around her waist. "Xavier's coming for dinner. I'm making meatloaf."

Tessa and Xavier have been together since sophomore year, and it's a rare night when he isn't here for dinner. Or waking up just in time for breakfast. At six-foot-seven and two hundred twenty five pounds, Xavier is a power forward for the basketball team and eats enough at dinner to feed a third world country. They are a match made in heaven because Tessa loves to cook. On special occasions, she loves to break out her *Abuela's* cookbook and experiment with elaborate Mexican dishes that I can't pronounce but will gladly eat. Her major is culinary arts, and she hopes to open her own restaurant someday.

"It smells great. Can I help?"

"Nope, but you can call your mom."

"I'd rather help."

Tessa smirks. "Stop that. Your mom is great."

"No argument here."

"*And* she finally gave me her kickass oatmeal raisin cookie recipe that I'm dying to try."

"You know, sometimes I step on the scale and wonder how I've gained twenty-five pounds since my freshman year. Then I remember I'm living with Rachael Ray."

Tessa laughs. "Whatever. Call your mom. Dinner will be ready in about twenty minutes."

Sighing tiredly, I take my backpack and head to my room. After quickly changing into a pair of yoga pants and a T-shirt, I grab my cell and climb onto my bed. In an instant, my calico cat joins me.

"Hey, pretty girl." I scratch behind her ears while she purrs and snuggles close. I've had Bangle since my senior year of high school. She's just one of the many reasons I'm thankful to no longer be living in the dorms. The separation anxiety was hard for both of us.

Snuggling time doesn't last long. Bangle suddenly jumps off the bed and trots out of the room, probably on the hunt for food. My suspicions are confirmed when I hear Tessa's voice echo from the kitchen.

"You know the rules, Bangle. No meatloaf for kitties."

I laugh and scroll through my phone, tapping on my mom's name.

"Hello?"

"Miss me?"

Mom laughs. "Is it that obvious?"

Growing up, it had just been the two of us in our tiny two-bedroom house. Only an hour separates us now, but Mom had still taken it hard when I decided to move away.

"Mom, we've talked every day, and I've only been gone a few weeks."

"I know. I just got used to having you around at Christmas."

We talk about my first day of classes and the six inches of snow that are predicted for tomorrow. Living in Indiana is always a crapshoot when it comes to winter weather. I'd worn a T-shirt and light jacket to class today. Tomorrow, I would need my snow boots.

"Have you met any cute guys?"

I automatically think about the soldier from the New Year's Eve party. It still surprises me how attracted I was, in spite of his military gear. Like a crazy person, I had actually looked around campus today, hoping to catch a glimpse of him. Unfortunately, he would have to be wearing his camo costume and thick face paint for me to recognize him.

"Oh, I hear a pause."

"There was no pause."

"Stephanie Lynn, lying to your mother is a sin."

"That hasn't worked since I was ten. What is it with you and your obsession with me finding a boyfriend?"

Mom sighs. "You just work too hard. You always have."

"A strong work ethic is an admirable trait."

"It is. I'd just like to see you have some fun this last semester, that's all."

Last semester. Such sweet words.

"With six classes and my job at the library, having fun is the last thing on my mind. I have to focus if I want to graduate in May."

"I know. You just can't wait to get out into the real world. But what have I always told you?"

I close my eyes and repeat my mother's mantra. "Don't be in such a hurry to work, because once you start, you'll never stop. Let yourself be young as long as you can."

"That's right. Just promise me you'll do something fun this last semester. Do something adventurous before you devote the rest of your life to your teaching career."

I know it's pointless to argue.

"Fine, I promise."

After we say goodnight, I think about my mom and her preoccupation with my lack of a social life. Getting married right after high school and becoming a mother, and a widow, by the time she was twenty had forced her to become an adult way too soon. She worked two jobs—one as the secretary at my elementary school and another as a freelance photographer on the weekends. Mom has worked hard all her life. She just wants me to experience all the things she missed.

Like I always do when I'm feeling anxious or confused, I reach into my shirt and pull out the silver ball chain. The cold metal of the dog tags against my skin serves as a constant reminder of the father I never knew. They are my only real connection to my dad and definitely my most prized possession.

When I think about my mom, and how lonely she has been for the past twenty-two years, I'm reminded why I hate the military so much.

And why I'm in no hurry to fall in love.

chapter

Two

Brandon

"Good afternoon and welcome to Women in Literature."

I can feel their eyes on me—even the professor's—and I know what they're thinking.

Why would a guy take this course? He has to be in the wrong class.

I'm not.

Unfortunately, the stares continue, so my brilliant plan to sit in the back of class and take a much-needed nap is shot to hell. I can sleep anywhere, but I can't sleep when I know I'm being watched.

I stifle a yawn and force myself to pay attention. My advisor had warned me that eighteen credit hours might be too much to handle, especially with my job at the coffee house and my 5:00 a.m. workouts, but I had ignored him and signed up for six classes anyway. And now, thanks to my one remaining humanities elective, I'm sitting in a Women's lit class, surrounded by girls.

Okay, maybe that part's not so bad.

The teacher drones as she goes over the syllabus. It doesn't look too tough. I like to read, which is why I hadn't complained when Mr. Ramirez, my advisor, suggested the course.

"It's either this or another foreign language," he'd said.

I'm already fluent in Spanish, German, and French. Do I really need to add another language to my résumé?

I glance around the room, and the girl to my right quickly turns her head away. I catch the slight blush of her cheeks.

I smirk. *Busted.*

She's cute, with her Peyton College sweatshirt and ponytail. But she's blonde. And tall. She also has a barbell in her ear. In other words, she's not the girl from the New Year's party, so I'm not interested at all.

That's what I call her—*the girl*—because I'm an idiot and didn't even ask for her name.

Like a man obsessed, I've searched in every class, stupidly hoping that by some cosmic coincidence she and I might have signed up for the same course. I had asked around after the party, but nobody could remember seeing a Disney princess in a yellow dress, which I still find unbelievable because she was the most interesting person there. She was pretty—not supermodel-like—but in a timeless, classic, girl-next-door way that's always attracted me.

And I can't forget the kiss.

I've had dreams about that kiss. Fantasies, really. So the fact that I haven't been able to find her is sort of pissing me off.

The professor assigns the first five chapters of *The Silence of Lambs*, and the class groans appropriately.

Five chapters? I wonder if I can get away with just watching the movie again.

I make a mental note to check Netflix just as a flash of brown catches my eye in the front row.

No way.

She's facing the teacher, so it's impossible to tell. I stare at the back of her head, hoping she'll feel the heat of my gaze and turn around.

Then she does.

Our eyes lock, and I can't believe how pretty she is. Or that she's sitting here, in my Women's lit class.

Cosmic coincidence for the win.

"I love that movie," she mouths.

Movie?

I must look confused, because she points at her shirt. I glance down at my own. Pictured on the front is Mandy Patinkin, circa 1987, with the immortal words 'Hello. My name is Inigo Montoya,' printed along the bottom.

I'm so happy to see her that I'm ready to just rip the shirt over my head and give it to her . . . but that'd probably be a little weird. Instead, I mouth "thanks," and we keep grinning at each other until she turns back toward the professor.

Disappointment floods me. *Does she even recognize me?* Granted, my costume that night wasn't very creative. It was a last minute invite, so I just grabbed what was handy, but maybe the black face paint was too much of a disguise.

Or maybe she hasn't been thinking about me at all.

The thought makes me a little nuts, so I dismiss it and spend the rest of class staring at the back of her head and wondering how I'm going to properly introduce myself.

But when the teacher dismisses us, the girl is out the door and gone.

38, 39, 40 . . .

My life has become a series of numbers, and today's magic number is 42.

Sweat rolls and my biceps burn while I grit my teeth and growl through the pain. Forty-two push-ups in two minutes is the *minimum*, and for my father, the minimum isn't good enough. It's nowhere near good enough.

44, 45, 46 . . .

Rigid back. Body straight.

Discipline. Strength.

But I'm too exhausted. Too frustrated. And I collapse against the cold ground before rolling over onto my back. With my chest heaving, I cover my eyes with my arm to shield the sun's glare.

"You're never going to pass that fitness test if you don't get your shit together."

My father's words echo in my ears. It was his way of pushing me. Molding me into what he always wanted to be.

The sweat dries on my face, making me shake despite the warmth of my hoodie. I do a few sit-ups to warm up before leaping to my feet.

And then I run.

It's my favorite thing to do when I'm stressed out or can't concentrate. Which is why earning the max score on my two mile run will be no problem at all, because running is all I've done lately.

My focus is shot, and I know she's the reason.

There's an outdoor track surrounding the football field, but I prefer to run on a wooded path just off campus. The rocky terrain leads straight uphill, which does more to build my endurance and strength than any number of push-ups could ever do. At the top of the hill is Rainbow Rock, a gray slab of granite that is decorated with names in various shades of ink and paint. Writing your name on the rock is a student tradition and something I've always planned to do but just haven't done.

With graduation just a few months away, I'll have to remember to do it soon.

I don't even bother to check my running time when I reach the top of the hill. I know it's good. It's always good. I just collapse on the ground and lean back against the rock, taking in the view. You can see the entire campus from here, and it looks nice, but nothing compares to home.

I miss Eastern Kentucky. A lot. And I miss my family. Going home for Christmas was great, but it's never long enough. It just makes me miss it more. And graduation won't help. While most graduates will be enjoying their last summer of freedom before starting their careers, I'll be headed to Georgia for three months of training.

If I can pass the fitness test.

Maybe it was a good thing the girl disappeared right after class. Now that I know she wasn't a figment of my imagination, maybe I can get my shit together and focus on my training schedule. Maybe those brown eyes won't haunt my dreams at night.

Maybe.

"Dude, you're missing the game!" Mark yells as I close the door behind me. The rest of my roommates barely acknowledge me. Their eyes are glued to the big screen television, cheering for Indiana.

We don't have a couch, but we have a sixty-inch plasma screen.

Priorities.

I can tell by their mood that Indiana is winning. The opponent isn't important—at least not to me. I know it's not Kentucky, so I don't care.

"Went for a run," I tell him, but his attention is back on the basketball game.

I shrug and kick my way through the dirty clothes and pizza boxes before heading to the shower. While living with a bunch of guys is good practice for the future, it isn't the ideal situation for a college student who actually needs to sleep at night. Our apartment is party central, which sucks for me but is the best I can do for now. Vince, my best friend, graduated in December and our apartment was just too expensive without a new roommate. When Mark suggested I move in here, I thought it was the perfect plan—until I realized I'd be sharing the space with four other guys. I'm grateful for the bed, so I don't complain.

After my shower, I decide to call my sister. Christian is four years older than me and practically raised me after our mom disappeared. She's a real mom now, with two little girls named Lucy and Lily, who call me Uncle Brandon.

It's weird.

But it's also cool.

Christian answers on the first ring. She sounds tired, and I tell her so.

"Of course I'm tired," she replies. "I am a single mother of five-year-old twins. I am the epitome of tired. What's your excuse?"

"How do you know I'm tired?"

"Because I know you."

She asks about school, and I ask about home. Not much changes in Applewood, our little coal-mining town deep in the hills of eastern Kentucky, but I ask anyway.

"Another mine closed today," Christian says. "Our town is dying and nobody seems to care.

You're smart not to come home after graduation, Brandon. There's nothing here."

"I'm not smart. I'm obligated. There's a difference."

"But you're happy to be obligated. I'm just . . . stuck."

"I thought you loved being a nurse?"

"I do, but my shift never ends," she says, sighing tiredly. "I am now a nurse, twenty-four hours a day. Combine all that with the girls, and I'm just drained. Mentally. Physically. Emotionally."

My guilt runs deep. She's way too young to carry this much weight on her shoulders. I should be doing more to help her.

"I want to help, Chris."

"You can. Just keep doing what Dad always tells us to do."

"Soldier on," I whisper.

It's our family slogan, my dad's personal mantra, and the phrase that echoes in my brain during my grueling training exercises.

"Stay focused. Stay determined. Follow your dream. Visit occasionally. Call me when you can. But live your life. That's what Dad would want. That's what I want. *That's* what you can do for me."

I smile in spite of my heavy heart. "How is he?"

"Today was a good day. He got a little agitated this afternoon when I told him he couldn't take the girls fishing. He'd forgotten it was January."

"So the memory lapses are getting worse."

"It just depends on the day. There are times he's as lucid as ever. Other days, he can't remember what he ate for breakfast. I made roast beef tonight, though. That made him happy."

My stomach growls in response, reminding me I forgot to eat.

"Well, that's because your roast beef is the best. Think he's in the mood to talk?"

"He's sleeping. So are the twins. Which means a very large glass of wine and a bubble bath are calling my name."

We say goodnight, and I set the alarm on my phone before climbing into the twin bed. For my six-foot-two frame, it's definitely not the best of sleeping arrangements, but again, I'm just grateful to have a place to crash.

My stomach growls again, but I'm too tired to care. I try to get comfortable and pull the blanket a little closer, but sleep doesn't come easily. My mind is too full of . . . everything. Family. School. Obligation.

Her.

And like always, her brown eyes are the last thing I see before I finally drift off to sleep.

chapter

Three

Stephanie

"Did you see the hook on that?" Xavier is practically jumping on the sofa.

"Yes, baby," Tessa says, rubbing his shoulder. "Amazing shot."

I roll my eyes at both of them before reaching for another cookie. We all love Hoosier basketball, and I'm thankful that my friends never make me feel like the third wheel whenever we watch the games together. Tonight, however, I'm just not feeling it.

At least the cookies are good.

"What's with you?" Xavier asks. "IU is beating Purdue by twenty."

I shrug. "It's just not the same with Zeller gone to the NBA."

Tessa snorts. "Oh, don't listen to her. This has nothing to do with the game. She's been grouchy ever since that New Year's Eve party."

"I have not!" *Have I?*

"Yes, you have. And it's perfectly understandable. If I'd been kissed by a hot guy at midnight—and I had no idea who he was and if I'd ever see him again—I'd be a grouch, too."

"What guy?" Xavier asks.

"Steph was kissed by some gorgeous G.I. Joe at midnight in the frat house library. Walked right up to her, kissed her, and then walked right out."

He turns to me with a confused expression on his face. "Frat houses have libraries?"

"This one does, and you might have known that if you'd explored other places in the house besides a bedroom."

Xavier smirks at his girlfriend. "You're right, this is about a guy."

"I know, right?"

Kill me.

He turns back to me. "So, G.I. Joe, huh?"

"He is *not* G.I. Joe. His costume was just camouflage and a lot of face paint."

"Like a soldier?" Xavier laughs loudly. "That's gotta suck for you. I mean, I know how much you hate them."

"It was just a costume, and I do not hate soldiers. Just the military in general."

"I don't see the difference."

I'm just about to explain the difference to him when Tessa suddenly jumps up. "Okay, I'm going to get more cookies. Does anyone need more milk?"

I take a deep breath. What should have been a fun night has turned into something serious and depressing, and I'm far too exhausted to deal with it. I stand up and toss the remote to Xavier.

"Actually, I'm going to skip the rest of the game and do some homework. Love you both."

"We love you, too," Tessa replies.

Xavier nods in agreement before shoving another cookie into his mouth.

I head to my room, where I send a quick hello text to Mom before snatching the worn paperback copy of *The Silence of the Lambs* off the shelf. I've read the book a dozen times, but if we're expected to read the first five chapters and write an analysis, I'm going to have to refresh my memory.

But instead of reading, all I can think about is him.

The guy in class was definitely cute, with his broad shoulders and cropped hair. Something about him made me want to smile back, so I did. It was only when his smile brightened that I noticed the dimples on his cheeks.

Dimples have always been my weakness.

Unfortunately, he's not the guy from the party who has set up permanent residence in my head.

Not that it matters.

I don't have time to find either of them interesting, even if one is a great kisser and the other loves *The Princess Bride*.

With a dejected sigh, I open my paperback and flip to chapter one.

By the end of the first week of classes, I'm completely stressed out and sleep deprived. Thankfully, it's Friday, and that means and I get to spend the rest of the afternoon in my favorite building on campus.

When it comes to part-time jobs, I really can't think of a better gig than working in the library. When I'm not checking-out or shelving books, I have all the time in the world to study. I've spent the last half-hour reading, but the twisted mind of Hannibal Lecter is too psychologically stimulating for someone running on three hours of sleep.

Giving up, I toss the paperback into my bag and search for a book cart. Shelving books is boring, but there are days when mindless productivity is exactly what I need.

Today is one of those days.

I roll the cart toward the Dewey Decimals. Glancing at the spine of the first volume, I look up to find its proper home on the shelf.

Of course, I'll need the ladder.

This stepladder is barely four feet off the ground and not nearly as fun as the last one. The memory of that night makes me smile as I climb.

Concentrate, Steph.

I've just placed the book on the shelf when my foot slips, causing my ankle to twist and the ladder to sway.

"Oh, sh . . ."

My curse is interrupted by my scream, and I tumble onto the floor, landing flat on my back. I groan as students rush to my rescue.

"Call 911!" a student yells.

"Do not call 911," I mutter.

I try to struggle to my feet, but my ankle protests, and I bite my lip before falling back onto the floor.

My stomach flips, and I close my eyes.

Please don't let me vomit in front of all these people.

Suddenly, I feel a pair of gentle hands framing my face. I open my eyes, and I'm greeted with dimples. And now that his face is inches from mine, I see he has gorgeous brown eyes to match his sexy dimples. Brown eyes that are so very, very familiar.

He smiles. "What is it with you, me, and ladders?"

Ladders. Brown eyes. Dimples.

Could it be?

"We really have to stop meeting like this," he says.

It could be!

"Did you hit your head?"

Did I? That would explain why I'm hallucinating at the moment. I mean, could the dimpled guy from my lit class be the same guy from the party? And am I the biggest idiot in the world for not making the connection?

"You look a little dazed," he says softly, his voice filled with concern. "I'd feel a lot better if you'd say something."

My laugh is shaky. "Sorry. And no, I didn't hit my head. Just my ass."

"What hurts?"

"My ankle."

"Can you sit up?"

"I . . . think so."

"Let's try."

He wraps his strong arms around me, helping me sit up so that I can rest my back against the bookshelf. I look around, and I'm grateful to see the little crowd of onlookers has disappeared.

He reaches for my shoe, and I wince in anticipation.

"What do you think you're doing?"

"I'm going to look at your ankle."

"Are you a doctor?"

"No, but I play one on TV."

"Seriously?"

"No. I just thought it was the natural thing to say."

I smirk. "Well, you are not touching my foot. It's just a sprain. I'll go home and take something for the pain. It'll be fine."

"Are you always this stubborn?"

"Yes, actually."

He laughs, and it's soft and sweet. "You should probably go to the student health center. Or the ER."

"Not happening."

"Okay. Will you at least let me take you home?"

"I am not getting into a car with you."

"Why not?"

"Because I don't even know your name."

"That didn't seem to bother you when you kissed me on New Year's Eve."

Excuse me?

"What are you talking about? You kissed me."

"That's not how I remember it at all."

"Well, then, your memory needs a little work."

"Fine. You can jog my memory while I drive you home."

Normally, I would have refused his offer. I pride myself on being strong, independent, and yes, a little stubborn. But he's cute. So much cuter without the face paint and head-to-toe camouflage. Not to mention, he has dimples, likes *The Princess Bride*, and gave me a midnight kiss that still curls my toes whenever I think about it.

I think about it a lot.

"Okay, you can drive me home . . . on one condition."

"What's that?"

"Tell me your name."

He smiles brightly and tips his imaginary hat.

"How do you do, ma'am. My name is Brandon Walker."

Despite my throbbing ankle, I laugh.

"I'm Stephanie James."

"It's nice to meet you, Stephanie James. Let's get you home."

"Okay, but I'll need to call Ms. Maria."

"Maria?"

"The librarian. She's at a faculty meeting. And I need to get my backpack. It's behind the counter."

"Okay."

Brandon climbs to his feet and places his arms around me. Before I can protest, he gently lifts me off the floor.

"You know, you don't have to carry me. I think I can hobble to the parking lot."

"That would be a long hobble. My truck is clear across campus."

"Of course it is." *How embarrassing is this?*

"Besides, your ankle could be seriously injured, and putting pressure on it could do lasting damage."

"I really don't think—"

"And this gives me an excuse to hold you in my arms, something I've wanted to do since New Year's Eve, so stop being stubborn."

Words fail me. I have no clever comeback. No witty response.

Brandon grins, and with a defeated sigh, I loop my arms around his neck.

"Are you Pre-Med?"

"Nope."

"Nursing?"

"Would you relax? It's just ibuprofen."

I sigh heavily and place the pills against my tongue. Brandon offers me a bottle of water to wash it down.

"Happy?" I ask after swallowing.

"Thrilled. Are you always this stubborn?"

"Haven't we already covered this? Yes, I'm very stubborn."

Brandon shakes his head and leans back against the couch. He glances around the living room. "Nice apartment. You live here alone?"

My cat chooses this moment to make her appearance. Bangle jumps onto the couch and immediately hisses at our guest.

"Umm . . . I guess not?"

I stifle my laughter. "No, I have a roommate. And this is Bangle. She doesn't like strangers."

On cue, Bangle hisses again. I don't even bother hiding my laughter this time.

"Sorry, she's protective, too."

Brandon chuckles nervously. "Obviously. Why did you name her Bangle?"

"Because I love The Bangles."

He frowns.

"Girl rock band from the 80s?"

"Oh, yeah. 'Walk Like an Egyptian,' right?"

"Right. If she had been a boy, I was going to call her Prince. But it wasn't meant to be."

"You must really like 80s music."

"I'm obsessed with the entire decade. The music, movies, television shows. I love it all." I know I probably sound like a crazy person, but it's best he knows now.

Now that she's been properly introduced, Bangle jumps down and makes her way toward the kitchen. I struggle to get comfortable with my swollen ankle propped up on the coffee table.

"How's the foot?"

Despite the ice pack, I can't ignore the fact that it seems to be getting bigger. "Maybe I should have gone to the ER or something."

"I suggested that."

"I know."

"We can still go."

"I'd really rather not. Can't we just . . . wait and see how it looks later?"

"Sure, especially since you said *we*." Brandon props his elbow up on the sofa and grins. "So, what are the odds that we're in the same lit class?"

"Women's Lit, no less."

"I couldn't believe it when I saw you sitting there. I'd asked around after the party, but nobody knew who you were. Someone said they thought were invited by one of the basketball players—"

"Xavier, yeah."

"But no one knew your name."

"Frat parties aren't my usual scene. Go figure."

"They aren't really mine, either, but it was New Year's Eve and I was bored. A buddy invited me. He thought it would be a good way to meet people."

"You mean girls."

"You sound jealous."

I scoff and shift on the couch.

"Believe me, Stephanie, you were, without a doubt, the most interesting person I met that night."

I wonder if it's a line, but it's a sweet one, so I decide to let it go.

"My friends call me Steph, by the way."

"Can I call you Steph?"

"Is that your way of asking if you can be my friend?"

He shrugs. "We can start there, sure. I don't think it'll last, though."

"Why not?"

"Well, I'm devastatingly charming, for one."

"And modest."

"Plus, that was some kiss. Do you really think two people who shared a kiss that hot can *just* be friends?"

It's the perfect opening for the question I've wanted to ask since the night of the party.

"If it was so hot, why did you run away?"

He has the decency to look appropriately ashamed. "I guess when it comes to pretty girls on library ladders, I'm just chickenshit. If it's any consolation, I haven't stopped thinking about you."

"I find that hard to believe."

"It's true. I felt like such an ass for not asking your name. That's why I was so excited to see you in class. I tried to catch you after, but you had disappeared."

"I'm an idiot. I didn't recognize you without your war paint and camo. I only noticed you at all because of your T-shirt."

He looks confused. "My shirt?"

I nod. "I'm obsessed with *The Princess Bride*. I can quote all ninety-eight minutes of the movie. It drives my roommate crazy whenever we watch it."

Brandon sighs dramatically. "Well, that proves it."

"Proves what?"

"Steph, we can't be friends."

"We can't?"

"Nope. Any woman who can quote the entire script of my favorite movie is marriage material. I should just propose right now, but I'd rather wait until I get a ring. Makes it more official."

I roll my eyes. I'm so not used to this level of flirtation. Or maybe it's just been a long time since anyone has paid this much attention to me. Either way, it's weird. Flattering, but weird.

"I think we should just start as friends and see how it goes."

He nods. "Fair enough, but I really think the unresolved sexual tension will be too much for us to handle, and you'll have no choice but to fall in love with me."

"I'll take my chances."

We share a smile just as a giggling Tessa walks through the door with Xavier close behind. Her laughter fades when she sees the two of us on the couch.

"What happened to your foot?" Tessa asks before turning her attention to the stranger on the sofa. "And who are you?"

Tessa can be a pit bull—loyal and a little scary.

"Sprained it, I think, and this is the knight in shining armor who brought me home."

Brandon springs to his feet and offers his hand to each of them while I make the introductions. The guys immediately start talking basketball while Tessa leans down to check on my ankle.

"Does it hurt?"

"Not much. Brandon forced me to take something for the pain."

"Brandon is cute."

"Brandon is G.I. Joe," I whisper.

Tessa's eyes widen and her mouth drops open. Without another word, she jumps to her feet, pulls Brandon into a hug, and rushes toward the kitchen. Within seconds, cabinet doors slam and pots and pans clang while she jabbers in Spanish.

Brandon slowly sits back down. "Is she okay in there?"

With a laugh, Xavier grabs the remote and collapses into the recliner. "Oh, yeah. All that noise you hear? That's happiness, man. Hope you're hungry."

I grin, because it's true.

Whenever Tessa is happy, her first instinct is to feed someone.

chapter four

Stephanie

"You're from Kentucky?" Tessa asks.

Brandon nods. "I grew up in a small town called Applewood. It's about thirty miles east of Pikeville."

"I played in a tournament there a few years ago," Xavier replies, scooping another helping of Spanish rice onto his plate. "That's *way* up in the Appalachian Mountains."

"Yeah, we're just a little coal mining town in the hills. Population is about eight hundred. There's a small hospital and a city hall. A few stores and restaurants, most of them locally owned."

I sit back and listen as my two best friends interrogate my . . . whatever he is.

This should be awkward—sitting at the kitchen table with my foot propped up on a chair while Tessa and Xavier grill Brandon on all the personal details of his life—but it's not at all. And if he's uncomfortable, it certainly doesn't show. He just keeps answering questions while Tessa continues refilling his plate. So far, I've learned he's a senior, majoring in computer engineering, and has a dad and an older sister who both live in Kentucky.

Brandon groans appreciatively as he takes another bite. "This is so good! I don't think I've ever had . . . what is this again?"

Tessa beams. "Turkey chimichangas. It's my *Abuela's* recipe."

Xavier slides his arm around his girlfriend's shoulder. "I don't even ask what she's cooking anymore. I don't ask what's in it. I just smile and eat."

"And you occasionally do the dishes," I reply.

Xavier groans a little.

"We should do that," Brandon says, before wiping his mouth with his napkin. He shoots me a grin before reaching for my empty plate. "How's the foot?"

I glance at my poor, elevated ankle. "It aches, but I don't think the swelling is getting any worse."

"That's a good sign." He nods toward the kitchen. "I'm going to help Xavier, and then I'll get some fresh ice for your ankle."

"Thanks."

Brandon and Xavier gather the dishes and head toward the kitchen. It isn't until we hear the faucet running that Tessa moves to the chair beside me.

"I like him," she says.

"I can tell. Since when do you dust off your grandmother's cookbook for traditional Mexican on a weeknight?"

"Well, this is a special occasion. You brought a nice guy home. That hasn't happened in . . . okay, it never happens."

I roll my eyes. "You are far too excited about this. But yes, he seems nice."

"But?"

"But I really know nothing about him."

"Well, Steph, there's this amazing thing called *dating*. It's when a guy and a girl invent things to do and places to go, all in an attempt to get to know each other. I realize this is a foreign concept since you haven't gone out in *forever*—"

"You're such a smartass."

"Seriously, it's been like a hundred years."

I sigh and shift uncomfortably in my chair. "Tessa, I have six classes and a part-time job. I don't have time to date."

"That's just an excuse to keep your nose buried in a book for the next four months. Besides, you know what they say about all work and no play?"

"Steph graduates in May?"

Tessa smirks. "That rhymed. Impressive."

"Thank you very much."

"All I'm saying is Brandon seems like a really nice guy. Why don't you get to know him *before* you totally dismiss the possibility?"

Before I can answer, the sound of breaking glass against linoleum echoes from the kitchen, followed by Xavier's muffled curse.

"Those boys are going to destroy my kitchen."

Tessa sprints out of her chair and runs toward the commotion. I'm still laughing when Brandon returns to the table moments later.

"I didn't do it," he says as he slides back into his chair. "But she threw me out anyway."

Of course she did, the little matchmaker.

"Yeah, she's territorial when it comes to her kitchen. She wouldn't be mad at you, anyway. You've charmed the pants right off her."

"Is that right?"

"That's right."

"And what about your pants?"

"My pants aren't coming off anytime soon."

We grin at each other, and it dawns on me that I'm actually flirting.

I never flirt.

"Well, I'm glad she likes me. I have a feeling I might need her help, what with you being so stubborn and all."

"Why would you need her help?"

"To convince you to go out with me."

My face heats, and I wonder if he can actually see my blush.

"Brandon, look—"

"We'll start small. Coffee? Tea? I know you're busy. I have classes and a job, too, but I'm willing to carve out thirty minutes in my hectic schedule to have coffee with you."

I have to admit, his sarcastic nature is kind of cute.

"Just coffee?"

"Yes. And when your ankle is no longer the size of Everest, maybe we can talk about dinner."

I grimace and look at my pitiful ankle. "It's not *quite* Everest . . ."

Brandon reaches for my hand, and I let him hold it. I mean, we've already kissed and he carried me across campus. Holding hands seems tame. He slides his fingers along mine, linking them. The sensation sends little jolts of electricity along my skin.

"When's your last class tomorrow?"

"I get out at three."

"There's this little coffee shop just off campus called The Daily Grind. If your ankle feels better, I'd love to meet you for coffee tomorrow after your class. Say 3:30?"

"Okay. If my ankle feels better."

His smile is triumphant. "You should probably give me your number . . . you know, just in case."

I roll my eyes, which causes him to laugh. Brandon releases my hand and digs his cell out of his pocket. I give him my number, which he immediately punches into his phone. Seconds later, I hear my ring tone coming from my backpack in the living room.

"And now you have mine," he says with a satisfied grin.

When I limp into The Daily Grind the next afternoon, I'm grateful to find the shop is nearly deserted. It can be a busy place—not just because it has the best coffee in town, but because of the awesome muffins the owner bakes each morning. It's a cozy coffee shop with round tables, padded booths, and loveseats and chairs nestled into the corners.

A few students with their laptops are scattered around the room, but Brandon isn't one of them, so I hobble to one of the loveseats and try to get comfortable. My ankle throbs, but the swelling isn't so bad today. Glancing down at my watch, I notice it's time to take more painkillers. I also notice that Brandon is ten minutes late.

Being stood up for a coffee date would be really embarrassing.

With a sigh, I unzip my backpack and dig for my meds. Maybe he's late, and maybe he is a flirt, but I have to admit he did take pretty good care of me yesterday. I find the ibuprofen bottle just as my cell vibrates. The message on the screen makes me smile.

You look pretty today.

I quickly look up, but he's nowhere to be found. Glancing out the window, I see a silver-haired guy riding a bike and a teenage girl walking her dog.

I send a text back.

Where are you?
Look at the register.

I do, and I laugh when I see him standing behind the counter, wearing one of the Grind's paisley aprons. He flashes his dimples and waves at me before turning his attention back to his customer.

I shake my head. *Those dimples are going to be the death of me.*

After the customer leaves, Brandon makes his way over.

"Nice apron. I never would have guessed paisley was your color."

"I know it's sexy, but please try to control yourself. I'm at work, after all."

"I'll try my best."

Brandon laughs. "I'm off in ten minutes. What would you like?"

"A muffin and a bottle of water, please."

"No coffee?"

"I hate coffee."

"Me, too." Brandon looks behind his shoulder. "Just don't tell Ms. Linda. She'll fire me."

"Ms. Linda?"

"The manager."

"Well, your secret's safe with me."

Brandon laughs and heads back to the register. I try to use the free time to study, but my textbook is boring compared to the guy behind the counter. I watch the way he interacts with the customers—giving each of them his dimpled grin and walking elderly customers to the door. It's sweet, watching the old ladies giggle like teenagers when they loop their arms through his as he walks them out.

After ten minutes, Brandon returns with two blueberry muffins and bottles of water.

"Bored yet?" he asks.

"Not at all. I'm curious, though. Why do you think grandmothers come to a college coffee shop?"

He sits down beside me. "Well, the shop has actually been here longer than the university. Plus, everyone knows Ms. Linda has the best muffins in town."

I grin, because it's obvious what brings the little old ladies to the shop, and it has nothing to do with Ms. Linda's muffins.

For the next hour, we bombard each other with questions. That's how I learn that he's been crashing at a friend's apartment.

"My roommate graduated and I couldn't afford the apartment by myself. I couldn't stand the thoughts of a dorm, so I'm staying with some buddies of mine. It's not so bad. There are five of us, so it's pretty much a constant party all the time, which sucks because I have to be up so early."

"How early?

"Five o'clock."

"*Five*? As in A.M.?

Brandon nods. "I work out each morning. It's mandatory."

I wonder why an engineering major would be required to exercise before dawn, but he changes the subject and asks about my family.

"I'm an only child. Mom lives in a small town just outside of Indianapolis."

"What about your dad?"

I take a deep breath and stare down at my hands. It's not that I mind talking about my father. I just never know how to explain it.

"I never met my dad. He was killed in Desert Storm before I was born."

Brandon reaches for my hand.

"I didn't know that. I'm sorry, Steph."

"Thanks." I squeeze his hand. "You know, they say it's hard to miss something you never had, but *they* are full of it. I miss my dad every single day."

"I understand. It must make you proud, though. Knowing he died defending his country."

I bristle. It's the same speech I've heard all my life. Some families probably find comfort in the fact that their loved ones died in combat. I've even had people tell me that I should consider it an honor.

I guess I'm selfish. I'd rather have my dad.

"Could we maybe talk about something else?"

Brandon nods and gives my hand a squeeze.

"Sure," he says. "I know! Let's talk about our first date. Is tomorrow good for you?"

I can't help but laugh. "I thought this was our first date."

"Absolutely not. *This* is muffins and water. First dates are supposed to be epic. It's the story we'll tell our children, and our grandchildren—"

"You know, you're pretty confident for a guy who wears a paisley apron."

He grins. "Tomorrow night. You, me, and my old VHS copy of *The Princess Bride*. I'll kick the guys out of the apartment, and we'll order a pizza."

"How about my apartment, my DVD, and I'll beg Tessa to cook?"

His dimpled smile melts my heart.

"It's a date."

chapter
five

Stephanie

Tessa meets me at the door. "You're home! How was your date?"

I stumble inside and drop my bag before hobbling toward the couch. "It wasn't a date, according to Brandon. It was muffins and water. But you'll be happy to know that our first official date is tomorrow night. And we're staying in, so if you don't mind, would you care to—"

"No problem. Xavier has a game."

"You're the best friend ever."

Her happiness fades. "I . . . really hope you still think so after I tell you what I need to tell you."

I'm instantly suspicious. I also notice her apron and a distinct aroma in the air.

"You're baking peanut butter cookies."

"Well, I know they're your favorite."

"Okay, what's going on?"

"I really wanted to feed you first."

"You can feed me later. Spill it."

She sits down next to me. My beautiful best friend, who never loses her cool or gets nervous about anything, looks a little pale.

"Steph, you know you're my best friend and that I would never, ever do anything to intentionally hurt you, right?"

"Which means you're about to hurt me."

"But not intentionally."

"Just spit it out, Tessa."

Taking a deep breath, she squares her shoulders and looks me in the eye.

"Xavier asked me to move in with him, and I said yes."

"Tessa, that's amazing! But why would . . ." my voice trails off as I realize how this news, as wonderful as it may be, could unintentionally hurt me. "Ah, the apartment. You want me to move out?"

Tessa's eyes grow wide. "No, of course not! His parents just bought the apartment building on Pike Street. The fancy one. You know, the place with the private terraces and fitness center?"

"You mean the one we call Paradise on Pike?"

"That's it! Xavier's allowed to live there rent-free as long as he stays in school, and his mom and dad love me, so they're all for it."

Tessa and Xavier have been dating since sophomore year, so moving in together isn't a complete shock. What's a little upsetting is the fact that they chose *now* to do it. It's just a few weeks into the semester—the first few weeks of their *last* semester—and they decide to make this kind of commitment now? After Tessa and I just made a commitment to our landlord in the form of a six-month lease?

"Steph, I know what you're thinking. I had every intention of staying through the summer. No one was more surprised than me when he asked me to move in with him." Tessa's eyes suddenly fill with tears. "I know it's selfish. You don't hate me, do you?"

With a sigh, I reach for my best friend and give her a tight hug. "It's not selfish and of course I don't hate you. I'm so happy for you. I'll just have to see if our landlord will let us out of our lease."

"You don't want to stay?"

"I can't afford the rent on my own."

Tessa frowns. "I know. I was thinking maybe you could find a new roommate. It would just be for a few months. I'll even help you look. It would help relieve my guilt."

"Don't feel guilty. I'll post an online ad or something and see what happens. Either way, it'll be fine."

"Promise?"

It will be fine or I will be homeless. No worries.

I force a smile. I'm not about to let the ball of anxiety that has just formed in the pit of my stomach ruin my best friend's excitement.

"I promise."

A sudden knock causes Tessa to beam brightly. I don't even have to wonder who is on the other side of the door.

"Come in," we yell in unison.

Xavier walks in slowly, cautiously, as if he's afraid a wild animal is on the loose. His eyes widen when he sees Tessa's tears.

"Do you hate us?" he asks.

I force another smile. I have a feeling I'll be doing that a lot over the next few days.

"How could I hate my two best friends?"

Xavier sighs with relief and plops down on the sofa.

We spend the rest of the evening with take-out pizza, peanut butter cookies, and some basketball game that I couldn't care less about. Deep down, I felt a little guilty. They're in love, and it's not surprising that they want to be together all the time. I'm happy for them, but at the same time, all I can think about is the fact that I will soon be sharing the sofa with a complete stranger.

Or you'll be homeless.

I wait until halftime before faking a headache and dragging my depressed ass to bed.

The next morning is cloudy and gloomy, which is ironic considering those two words perfectly describe my mood.

To say this is the worst day for a first date is the understatement of the year.

Throughout the morning, I seriously consider texting Brandon and faking the flu, but something stops me. The fact is that I like him. A lot. Which is weird because it usually takes me much longer to feel comfortable around someone. Tessa found the perfect guy in Xavier, but I've never been lucky when it comes to dating. Most college guys are jerks. Or liars. Or both.

Brandon is different. Instinctively, I know this, and that's what stops me from breaking our date.

I've spent the afternoon on the couch with my laptop, scrolling through ads on Peyton Central, our school's equivalent to Facebook. Students can check e-mail, sell used textbooks, browse for campus internships, and sometimes, find a new roommate.

So far, I'm unimpressed.

Oh, there are plenty of eager hopefuls. Some even posted pictures. And while my 80s-loving heart is impressed with the ad that reads, 'Seeking roommate who likes to watch *Back to the Future* and listen to old school Mellencamp,' I just can't help but think the crafty bastard, whose name is BigDaddy21, is probably just looking for a girlfriend.

Giving up, I close my laptop and head to the kitchen to finish dinner. Tessa made lasagna, so the apartment already smells like heaven. As I place the garlic bread in the oven, the depressing thought hits me that, very soon, I'm going to be cooking my own meals.

I have a feeling there's going to be a lot of take-out in my future.

The knock at the door jerks me right out of my pity party. I limp my way through the living room and open the door.

"Hi."

"Hey." He's wearing his Inigo Montoya T-shirt and holding a pretty bouquet of wildflowers. He looks a little nervous. "Umm . . . I couldn't decide between these and roses, but my dad always said that you should bring flowers to a girl any chance you get, so I'm . . ."

He's babbling, and it's adorable. I decide to put him out of his misery and reach for his hand, pulling him inside.

"Wildflowers are my favorite."

His face immediately relaxes. "Yeah?"

"Yes."

I lead him into the kitchen, where I find a vase and fill it with water. "This was really sweet of you. Thank you."

Over dinner, we talk about school. I'm surprised to learn his schedule is just as horrible as mine, and just like me, he has to graduate in May. Summer classes are not an option.

"I just want to be done. One last summer of freedom before I start teaching."

Brandon nods. "I understand. I'm headed to Georgia right after I graduate."

Before I can ask what's in Georgia, he asks about my future plans.

"I really want to teach English."

"Here?"

"Anywhere. Hopefully close to home, but I'll go wherever there's a job."

Dinner is delicious, of course, and we each send a quick text to Tessa to thank her for cooking before we head to the living room. I pop the DVD into the player and hand him the remote.

He pulls me toward the couch. "Do you cry?"

"What do you mean?"

"You know, when Westley supposedly dies, or when Buttercup marries Prince Humperdinck. Do you cry?"

"She doesn't technically marry him, if you remember."

Brandon chuckles and helps me get comfortable on the sofa. My ankle doesn't hurt nearly as much now, but he insists I prop it up anyway.

For the next ninety minutes, we watch our favorite movie as if it's the very first time. It *feels* like the first time, because I'm watching it with someone who truly loves it as much as I do. During the movie, our bodies drift closer, until Brandon finally takes my hand while wrapping his other arm around me. I snuggle deep into his arms without taking my eyes off the television.

It should be weird, but it's not.

"I could never go out with someone like Buttercup," Brandon says in the middle of the movie. "She has no faith whatsoever."

I laugh. "Well, I could never date someone who disappears for years and lets me believe he's dead."

"So, who could you date?"

You. The thought is immediate. Thankfully, it remains a thought and the word doesn't escape my mouth.

"Let's just watch the movie, okay?"

He smirks and turns his attention back to the screen.

"I have to admit . . . I sort of want to punch Westley in the face every time he says 'as you wish.' I never understood why he couldn't just say 'I love you' like a normal person."

"Oh, I don't know," I reply. "Maybe because he was chickenshit . . . kind of like the guy who kissed a girl on a library ladder and then ran out of the room like he was on fire."

Brandon chuckles. "Who knew Westley and I had so much in common?"

The evening passes quickly. Too quickly for me. I'm too comfortable, wrapped in his arms as if we've been together for years. I sneak a peek at him as he watches the sword fight between Inigo Montoya and the Six-Fingered Man.

"You're missing the end," he whispers.

Busted. "Sorry."

At the end of the movie, when the grandfather talks about the five most passionate and pure kisses, I can literally feel Brandon's gaze on me.

I tilt my head in his direction. "You're really missing the end."

He pulls me closer as his eyes flicker to my mouth, and I nearly laugh because this moment is completely cheesy and predictable.

But I don't laugh. I don't even breathe.

I'm impatient, so I lean in, kissing him softly. Weaving my fingers into his hair, I pull him closer. Brandon groans and presses his body against mine. He's soft and warm and I feel it again . . . the butterflies or somersaults or whatever you want to call it that lets me know that this isn't just an ordinary kiss, and Brandon is no ordinary guy.

And I know, deep in my heart, that I'm in trouble.

"You know, you never answered my question," Brandon says.

The movie ended an hour ago, but we haven't moved from the couch. I've never understood why couples make out in the backseats of cars. Couches are so much more comfortable.

"Which question was that?"

"Who could you date?"

"Hmm." I pretend to ponder. I mean, really, shouldn't it be obvious by now? "Someone who is kind-hearted. Someone who walks old ladies to the door of the coffee shop. Someone who looks sexy in a paisley apron."

He smiles and twirls a lock of my hair around his finger. "What about a Kentucky Wildcats fan? Could you date one of those?"

It's a fair question, considering my Indiana roots and my love for Hoosier basketball.

I wrinkle my nose. "I suppose."

"Good to know."

We both laugh, and he buries his face against my neck. He really likes my neck.

"Honestly, there's only one type of guy I could never date."

Brandon lifts his head. "And what type is that?"

"I could never, ever date a soldier."

His entire body stiffens.

"You won't date a soldier?"

His voice is flat. Robotic.

"No, I won't."

"What do you have against soldiers?"

"I have nothing against soldiers."

"But you just said—"

I shake my head. "I have nothing against soldiers. It's the military I have a problem with."

"What's the difference?"

I gaze into his deep brown eyes. They look tortured now. Sad. And I have no idea why. *Have I offended him?* Maybe his dad was in the military or something. Surely he would have mentioned that. Wouldn't he?

"Do we really have to talk about this right now?"

"I . . . think we do."

I sigh heavily. "The difference is that I can admire and respect the people who put their lives on the line for me. I just don't think young men and women should be forced to choose between their country and their family."

Brandon blinks. "But the military doesn't make them choose. No one's been drafted since Vietnam."

This is getting deep. And uncomfortable.

"Brandon, maybe we should just watch another movie."

"This is because of your dad, isn't it? Because he got killed in Desert Storm."

"Well . . . yes. Don't you think that's a good reason?"

He lets go of me, and I immediately miss him.

"Your father died doing something courageous and brave. Something he felt was his duty. That should give you comfort. You should be proud, Steph. You should be honored."

I leap to my feet. If there's one thing I can't stand, it's being told how *honored* I should feel that I never had the chance to meet my father.

"My dad was killed by friendly fire when his helicopter was shot down over Khafji, so no, I don't feel honored. I feel robbed. I grew up without a father, and my mom was a widow at the age of twenty. *Twenty.* So you'll have to forgive me if I don't feel honored."

I take a deep breath and try to calm down. The last thing I want to do is cry in front of him.

"You really feel this way? You really hate the military that much?"

"I really do."

He looks at me as if he's seeing me for the first time. He nods once and rises to his feet.

"I should go," he whispers.

What?

"You don't have to," I tell him, but he's already reaching for the door.

"I have to get up at five, Steph. I'll talk to you later."

I watch him go. I have no idea what happened in the past five minutes. No idea why he's reacting this way. Clearly, I've insulted him. I just wish I knew why.

So much for our first date.

chapter six

Brandon

Sweat rolls down my face as I groan loudly, giving the bag one last quick kick. I haven't kickboxed in months. Now I remember why. Everything burns. Everything hurts. And the pain is welcome. It reminds of what a dumbass I am.

With a tired grunt, I collapse against the mat.

I'm so pissed at myself. And at her. But most of all, I'm pissed at my stupid heart because it was leading me down a path I have no business going down, and it was *this* close to convincing me to make the biggest mistake of my life.

What was I thinking? It's not as if I have time for a girlfriend. Hell, I barely have time to sleep. And in four months, I'll have even less time. I'll be training all summer. After that, only God knows where I'll be.

Not that it matters.

And maybe that's the part that pisses me off the most, because it never mattered. From the very beginning, I had zero chance.

Zero.

I close my eyes and think back to the few conversations we've had.

Did she really have no idea?

"Dude, you just beat the shit out of that bag."

The voice is vaguely familiar, but I don't care enough to actually open my eyes.

"Isn't that what it's for?"

"Well, yeah, but I'm not sure how I feel about Steph dating somebody with so much rage. She's a sweet girl and—"

My eyes snap open at the sound of her name. I look up to find Xavier standing over me. He's sweating like a pig, too. Probably just came from practice.

"Brandon, man, you look like hell."

"Well, that's exactly how I feel, so . . ."

He offers me a hand, and I take it, because my legs are jelly. Standing hurts, but again, that's okay. I need the constant reminder that I'm an idiot.

"Thanks. You'd never know I run two miles a day."

Xavier hands me a clean towel. "Running and kicking are two entirely different things. Different muscles. Different techniques."

I don't really care, but I don't want to be rude. "Yeah. Well, thanks for the towel. I'm just gonna hit the shower."

I've just turned to go when I feel his hand on my shoulder.

"Seriously, man. Steph is a sweet girl and one of my best friends. I need to know."

I sigh and turn back around. "Need to know what?"

"Are you always this pissed off or are you just having a bad day?"

Xavier's a good guy, but it's not like I can really talk to him. Anything I say will be told to Tessa, who in turn will tell Steph.

It's like I'm in high school all over again.

"Just a bad day, Xavier. That's all it is."

"Good."

We make plans to play basketball sometime before I head to the shower. The hot water does very little to ease the soreness in my muscles, but I don't mind the pain. It'll remind me to keep my mind on my obligations and off the pretty girl who is destined to hate me.

Just because I'm a soldier in the U.S. Army.

"What's wrong?" Christian asks.

I thank Ms. Linda for the muffin before heading for a secluded booth in the back of the Grind.

"Can't a brother call his sister twice in one week? Why do you assume something's wrong?"

"Because I know you."

I roll my eyes. That's her answer for everything these days. The sad part? It's totally true, which is probably why I'm calling my sister to get advice about a girl.

"Maybe I'm just homesick. That's possible, you know."

Dead silence.

"Fine. I need your advice."

For the next ten minutes, I spill my guts. I tell my sister about the New Year's Eve kiss and meeting Steph again in class. I tell her about *The Princess Bride* and Steph's big brown eyes and how she's literally all I can think about. And then I tell her about Steph's dad, and the war, and how she despises anything that has to do with the military.

"Brandon, surely you can understand why."

"Not really, no. I think it's immature and irrational to hate soldiers who put their lives on the line for her each day."

"Lord, now you sound like Dad," she mumbles. "Did she say she hates *all* soldiers? Did those words actually come out of her mouth?"

"No. She just said she could never date one."

Dead silence. Again. My sister is never speechless.

Finally, she sighs. "Oh. I see."

"You see what?"

"This is not good, Brandon."

"What? What's not good?"

"You really like this girl."

"And that's bad?"

"I think it's terrible."

Unbelievable.

"Thanks a lot, Christian."

I hang up without even saying goodbye.

Now that I'm completely pissed off with pretty much everyone and everything, I toss my uneaten muffin in the nearest garbage can and head out into the chilly January air. What I really need to do is study, but the textbook I need is back at the apartment, and I'm in no mood to deal with my roommates. A run would be good, but since my kickboxing workout kicked my ass, I decide to walk up to Rainbow Rock instead. It's the one place on campus where I can find a little peace.

I walk . . . *slowly*, and I'm sort of regretting my decision to hike up the mountain until I reach the top of it.

She's there, sitting against the rock. Her hair is in a ponytail, which gives me a perfect view of her neck.

I really love her neck.

Our kisses have been fairly innocent, but there was this one spot along the column of her throat that, when I kissed it, she would sigh softly. If I kept kissing it, those sighs would eventually turn into moans.

I really love the moans, too.

"Are you just going to stand there and stare at me?"

Steph turns her head in my direction. Her brown eyes are sad and tired, and I know I'm the reason. I also know that, in this moment, at the top of this mountain, it doesn't matter if she hates the color of camouflage.

I want her, and just maybe, she wants me, too.

"I can think of worse things to do than to stare at the prettiest girl I've ever seen."

"Right."

"You are, Steph."

"Then why do you keep running away from me?"

I walk closer to the rock and sit down beside her. "I just . . . needed some time to think, that's all."

She pulls her knees close to her chest and places her cheek against them, gazing thoughtfully at me. A lock of brown hair has fallen into her eyes. I reach over, gently brushing it away.

"I guess I owe you an apology. I know I offended you in some way, and for that I'm sorry."

"It's okay, Steph."

"No, it's not. I get a little worked up, and I'm well aware that my opinion of the military isn't a rational one. But I can't help how I feel. I just can't support something that stripped me of the chance to know my father. Can you understand that?"

And for a moment, I can.

It's a memory—deep, dark, and filled with grief—but it's important I tell her. Because in a weird way, I do understand. I get how you can attach an irrational response to childhood trauma, even if it doesn't make sense to anyone else.

I clear my throat. "I loved caramel apples when I was a kid. It was the night before Halloween, and I talked my mom into making them. She went to the store to buy butter and sugar, and she never came back. I was ten years old."

"Oh, Brandon—"

"I blamed myself, of course. Kids are good at that. I just didn't understand. From that day on, I hated Halloween and caramel apples. Still do. It's not rational, and I know that, but old habits are hard to break, and childhood wounds run deep."

Steph slides closer and places her head on my shoulder. Her hair smells like peaches and cream, and I close my eyes, burning the scent into my memory.

I never want to forget it.

"I'm sorry you lost your mom."

"I'm sorry you lost your dad."

The winter wind blows across our faces. She's wearing a jacket, but she trembles anyway. I wrap my arms around her, and she slides closer. For the first time in hours, I finally feel myself relax.

This isn't normal. It can't be.

"Why is this so easy?" I ask her.

She laughs a little. "It wasn't so easy last night. Why did you get upset? I mean, we haven't talked much about your dad. Was he in the military or something?"

I close my eyes. *Have I never mentioned I'm in Army ROTC? How has that never come up in conversation? And what about the New Year's Eve costume? Did she really think the camo and war paint was just some random disguise?*

"My dad served two tours in Vietnam."

Her eyes widen. "Vietnam?"

"Yeah, Dad's sixty-four. My folks waited until he was retired before having kids. Mom always said she didn't want to be a single mother, and she would have been. Dad was married to the military." I laugh, but it's not at all humorous. "It's ironic. She waited until he was retired, and *then* she left him."

"That's crazy."

"Welcome to my world."

"Have you seen her since?"

I shake my head. "She's called a few times. I have nothing to say to her. My sister raised me. Dad . . . tried his best, but military discipline and parental discipline are two very different things. He had a hard time distinguishing between the two."

"He was on hard you," she says softly.

"He wasn't cruel, but he was tough. Very structured. Very rigid. I rebelled hard when I was a teenager. We clashed a lot."

"Is your relationship better now?"

Up until three years ago, my relationship with my father was the best it had ever been, due to the fact that I was doing exactly what he wanted and joined the Army. But now . . .

"I'm sorry. Is that too personal?"

I smile sadly and shake my head.

"It's just a little hard to answer, that's all."

She nods as if she understands before placing her head back on my shoulder.

"We should go," I say after a while. "The sun's going down. It's just going to get colder."

"Okay."

Taking her hand, I help her to her feet, and I don't let it go, not even when we're past the rocky terrain and back on the concrete sidewalk that stretches through campus.

Steph looks up at me. "Are you still mad?"

"No. I understand why you feel the way you do. I don't agree with it, but I understand it."

"That's fair," Steph says. Then she laughs. "But you know what's not fair? Having to find a new roommate."

"Who's looking for a new roommate?"

"I am. Tessa and Xavier are moving in together. With utilities, our place is about $600 a month. I need to find a roommate because I can't afford it by myself. Plus, I'd like to stay there because our building is one of the few that allows pets. I can always move back home with my mom, but then I'll be commuting. That thought doesn't exactly thrill me."

I quickly do the math in my head. I could totally afford that.

"Umm, Steph?"

"I placed an ad on Peyton Central, hoping someone out there needs a place to live, but the only people who replied are guys probably looking for a girlfriend and—"

"Steph, I—"

"It's just completely depressing and I really don't want to talk about it anymore. Could we go get some hot chocolate or something? It's really cold."

It's too perfect. How can she not see how perfect it is?

I stop in my tracks and pull her close, wrapping my arms around her.

"Better?"

She sighs and snuggles against my chest. "So much better."

I hold her tight and wonder how my shitty day has, within moments, become the best day ever.

I need a place to live. Steph needs a roommate. If I can keep my hands to myself, I could show her that I'm a good guy. A decent guy. Despite the fact that I'm committed to the United States Army. Despite the fact that I'm a soldier. Her opinion of military life is an emotional response to a heartbreaking situation, and I can't blame her for feeling the way she feels.

But what if I can change her mind?

For me.

It's in this moment that I accept the fact that I care for this girl far more than I should. We just met a few weeks ago, and we barely know each other.

But what if we *got* to know each other?

They say you don't truly know someone until you've lived under the same roof with them. Yes, I'm twisting that philosophy to justify what I'm about to do, but in this moment, with this girl, I am willing to take the chance.

Even if it means keeping my mouth shut about my life as a soldier.

For now.

chapter
seven

Stephanie

Flurries swirl in the breeze as we continue on our way to the apartment. I find it strange, because it doesn't seem cold enough to snow.

Maybe that's because he hasn't let go of you since you left the mountain.

"Steph, I can't believe you posted on that website. Are you insane?"

"No, I'm desperate."

"And I'm hurt."

Now what did I do?

I look up at him and frown. "Hurt? Why?"

"Have you forgotten that I'm looking for a place to live?"

I'm stunned. I *had* forgotten. But even if I'd remembered, I don't know that having Brandon as a roommate is the answer to my problem. It could actually *create* problems, and that's the last thing either of us need.

"Brandon, I'm not sure the two of us living together would be a good idea."

"Why not?"

"Well, for one thing, we don't know each other that well."

"I think you know me a little better than you know the complete strangers on that website."

Good point.

"It's very important that I graduate on time."

"And you think having me as a roommate would keep that from happening?"

"I think you could be a very, very distracting roommate."

"Oh. I understand." He laughs softly and walks away.

I have to practically run to catch up with him. "You do?"

"Yep."

He doesn't say another word as we walk toward my building. When we reach the apartment, he grabs my hand and swiftly pins me against the door. His face is just inches from mine.

"You like me."

Brandon brushes his nose against mine. It's such a sweet, innocent gesture, but it's enough to make me shake in my snow boots.

"Yes, I like you. I like you a lot."

"I like you, too, Steph. A lot. Far more than I should, I'm afraid."

He sighs and buries his face against my neck. He tenderly kisses the skin there, and a soft moan escapes my lips.

"See, Brandon? That's why I'm afraid that living together, where we will be free to touch or . . . whatever . . . anytime we want, might not be the best idea if we want to keep our eyes on the prize."

Brandon raises his head and grins slyly. "Or *whatever*? Whatever could you possibly mean?"

I roll my eyes. "Of course that's the part you heard."

He chuckles and lowers his head, kissing me gently.

"I understand, Steph. You're afraid I won't be a gentleman."

"No. I'm afraid I won't want you to be."

"And I can't promise that I will be, so maybe you would be safer with a complete stranger."

"Brandon, that's not what—"

"It's okay. Because you're right. The one thing neither of us can afford to lose is our focus."

I can hear the defeat in his voice, and it makes my heart ache.

"But we're okay?"

He kisses my forehead. "We're great."

"Good." I smile. "Do you want to come in? Tessa's probably out with Xavier. I could make that hot chocolate?"

He nods, and I lead him inside. For the rest of the evening, Brandon laughs and talks and pretends everything is okay between us, and maybe it is. We're still getting to know each other, so I'm not very in-tune with his moods just yet, but I can't help but feel that he's forcing it, and that maybe I truly disappointed him.

And that's the last thing I'd ever want to do.

"You're an idiot."

Leave it to my best friend to confirm my worst fears. We're spending the afternoon on Tessa's bedroom floor, wrapping her breakables in bubble wrap and trying not to think about the fact that this weekend is the last we'll spend together under the same roof.

"He drives me crazy, Tessa."

"And this is a bad thing?"

"It's a bad thing when I need to—"

"If you say 'keep my focus' I swear I'll scream."

I snap my mouth closed.

"Steph, you've spent your entire college career focused on one thing and one thing only— graduating with honors. You don't socialize. You don't party. You never date. You don't do anything fun or adventurous. And that's fine if it makes you happy. But I can't help but wonder if you're going to graduate and not really know yourself at all. We are supposed to use these years to be creative, to be daring, and you've spent four years with your nose stuck in a book."

"And your idea of being daring is for me to live with a guy I barely know?"

Tessa smirks.

"Okay. For a moment, let's pretend that's the issue here. What's the difference in living with Brandon and living with a complete stranger you met on the internet?"

I stare down at my fingers. Tessa knows me better than anyone, and she's always willing to call me on my bullshit excuses.

"There's no difference."

"Exactly. Inviting him to live here is actually the perfect solution. You know him. You like him. He's a nice guy. I know I'll feel better about moving out if I know he's your roommate, and I bet your mom will feel the same way. I mean, have you seen his biceps? He could do some serious damage to anyone who tried to hurt you."

I laugh. "Sure, let's ask my mom how she feels about me moving in with my muscular boyfriend."

Tessa pops one of the bubbles on the wrap, making me jump.

"Boyfriend?"

"Figuratively speaking," I mumble.

She laughs gently and places the last of her picture frames into the cardboard box. With a sigh, she turns toward me and reaches for my hand.

"Do you know what I think? I think you're afraid. You're afraid of the way he makes you feel, and if you're forced to live with him, you'll have to face it head-on. Do I think you should share a bedroom? Of course not. This is new. Boundaries should be set. Rules should be established. And then *you* can decide when and if you want to break them. And then you must call me immediately after because I will want *all* of the details."

We laugh and get back to work. By the end of the afternoon, the only thing that remains is the small dresser and bed—a gift for the new roommate. A lump forms in my throat as I look around at the bare bedroom walls.

I'm not sure what I was expecting when she announced she was moving, but I don't think I imagined it happening so soon.

The two of us spend the rest of the day on the couch with the remote and an 80s movie marathon. As soon as Kevin Bacon stops dancing at the end of *Footloose*, she heads to the kitchen to start dinner.

Our last supper. In this apartment, anyway.

It's bittersweet, for sure. Tessa and I have been joined at the hip since our freshman year in the dorms. Even when Xavier came into the picture, nothing really changed. I know, deep down, that she and I will always be best friends, but I think we both realize that things are going to be very different from now on.

Maybe that's not such a bad thing.

While Tessa thinks college is supposed to be daring and fun, I've always believed these years are about growing up and finding your place in the world. Tessa's place is with Xavier . . . in their kitchen, and in their apartment.

My place is here, for now.

For dinner, she breaks out her grandmother's cookbook to make Red Chile Chicken Enchiladas. Together, we bake peanut butter cookies, which are two dishes that normally wouldn't go together, but she is determined to make all my favorites, one last time.

"I'm a terrible best friend," she says over dinner.

"Why would you say that?"

"You're going to starve when I'm gone."

I laugh and take the last bite of my enchilada. "Yes, you should be completely ashamed of yourself. Whatever will I do?"

Her face brightens. "I could leave you my *Abuela's* cookbook! You could practice cooking for Brandon—"

"No, Tessa."

"I'm just saying."

We eat, laugh, and talk until the wee hours of the morning, and when it's finally time to sleep, we hug as if our lives depend on it.

I manage not to cry until I reach the sanctuary of my room.

Hours pass. I try to sleep, but it's useless. My mind is spinning with doubts, and a little nagging voice keeps telling me I'm an idiot.

Tomorrow night, it'll just be me and Bangle in our little apartment.

In the quiet darkness of my bedroom, the reality of that hits me hard, to the point I'm half-tempted to call my mom. But it's far too late—or early—depending on your perspective.

I'll call her tomorrow, when I can actually carry on a conversation without crying.

What are you so afraid of?

The question echoes in my head, and no matter how hard I try, I can't come up with an answer. Maybe Tessa's right. Could I really be so afraid of my feelings for Brandon that I don't trust us to share an apartment? Will having him this close be too much—for both of us?

Desperate for a sign, I climb out of bed and reach for my laptop. Bangle joins me back under the covers as I log on to Peyton Central.

No new messages.

With a disgusted sigh, I place the computer back on the floor.

I close my eyes, begging for sleep to take me. I've nearly drifted off when my phone vibrates on the nightstand. I reach for it, and the message on the screen makes my heart skip a beat.

Brandon has actually typed out the lyrics to "In Your Room" by The Bangles, which is both amazingly awesome and disturbingly appropriate.

And now, I'm wide awake again.

Still, it isn't until the Indiana dawn begins to peek through my window that I finally find the courage to send him a reply.

Excellent song choice.

Did I wake you?

No. Can't sleep.

I'm getting ready to go for a run. Want to join me?

Not on your life.

He replies with a smiley emoticon. I take a deep breath, and my fingers tremble as I type out what could quite possibly be the most important text of my life.

Move in with me?

It takes more than an hour to get a reply, but it's well worth the wait. With three little words, Brandon gives me the only sign I need.

As you wish.

"Who can tell me some of the underlying themes in our excerpt from *Silence of the Lambs*?"

Today's class has been torture. Not because I didn't do my homework or because I'm unprepared to answer the professor's questions about theme and symbolism. It's torture because of the cute guy sitting next to me. The same guy who hasn't stopped touching me since class began.

My new roommate.

He's subtle about it. A simple brush of his fingers against mine. A gentle massage along the nape of my neck. Sweet, innocent touches that make it impossible to concentrate on anything except the fact that his hands are on me.

When did I become such a girl?

I look over to find his eyes fixed on the professor, but the little smirk on his face assures me that he knows exactly what he's doing.

After another hour of torturous touches, the professor assigns next week's reading assignment and dismisses the class. We practically bolt out the door.

"Follow me."

I nod, and Brandon takes my hand. I don't even ask where we're going. We head down the hallway and through a corridor that leads to more classrooms—all of which seem to be empty. He quickly pulls me into one of the dim rooms and kicks the door closed behind us before leading me to the teacher's desk. Lifting me up, he gently places me on top and steps between my legs. We're laughing until he lowers his head, trailing his lips down my neck and along my jaw. I groan, which makes him do the same.

We kiss until we're breathless.

"What's this?" Brandon whispers, and I feel his fingers trail along the chain around my neck. Reaching down into my shirt, I pull out my dad's silver tags.

"I've never noticed these before."

"I don't wear them all the time."

He carefully examines the inscription. "William James."

"Mom called him Billy. Besides some old pictures and a framed flag, it's really the only connection I have to my dad. I like to wear it when I'm stressed out or worried. It . . . makes me feel better."

Brandon smiles and runs his fingers along the silver metal before slipping the chain down my shirt, letting it fall back into place.

"I'm impressed. You didn't even sneak a peek."

"Thought about it. It just didn't seem appropriate." He grins and laces his fingers with mine. "Since you're wearing the tags today, I'm assuming you're worried, and I bet it has something to do with our living arrangement."

I sigh deeply. "A little, yes."

"Why?"

I decide to prove my point.

"What's our reading assignment for next week in Women's Lit?"

His blank stare is my answer.

"See! I don't know, either. We literally just left class, and I can't remember one thing the teacher said because your hands were very, very distracting. *You* are very, very distracting."

Brandon leans down and kisses just below my ear.

"Sorry," he whispers.

"No, you're not."

"How do you know?"

"Because I'm not sorry, either."

He chuckles and helps me down. Taking my hand, he leads me out of the building and into the chilly afternoon. About three inches of snow is on the ground, but thankfully, the sidewalks are clear.

"We can make this work," Brandon says as we walk. "I know we can. We just have to set some boundaries, that's all."

"That's what Tessa said, too."

"She's right." He looks down at his watch. "She's moving her stuff this afternoon?"

"Yeah, Xavier and some guys from the team were loading her boxes as I left for class."

He nods. "I should probably start packing, too. I don't have much. It'll probably take just a few boxes."

"And you don't need a dresser or bed. Tessa left hers."

"Sweet. What size bed?"

"It's a queen, I think. That okay?"

Brandon laughs. "I've been sleeping on a twin, so anything is better than that."

It's become a habit, him walking me to my apartment. *Our* apartment, now, I guess. So I'm not surprised when we find ourselves standing in front of it.

"What are you thinking about?" he asks as we step inside.

"Thinking it's sort of scary how I just blindly follow you anywhere."

A thoughtful expression crosses his face, and he steps closer, taking my hands in his.

"I'm glad you trust me enough to do that," he says, his voice soft and deep. "I can't lie, though. This is new territory for me, and I could really mess it up. But I care a lot about you, and I can't promise I'll make the most rational decisions, so when it comes to us—not as roommates, but as *us*, I'm following your lead."

There's no need to read between the lines. He's telling me, right here in the entryway of my apartment—of *our* apartment—that when it comes to our relationship, I'm calling the shots.

"Maybe we can lead each other," I tell him.

chapter eight

Brandon

Mark and my other roommates help me unload before heading off to the basketball game. Normally I'd go with them, but I need to get unpacked.

At least, that's what I tell them.

After giving me the grand tour, Steph went to class while I began the process of turning Tessa's old room into my own. I wasn't lying when I said I didn't have much stuff. Knowing I was headed straight to Fort Gordon after graduation, I had packed light for my last semester at Peyton. Everything made it into two cardboard boxes and a suitcase. I also have my Army-issued green duffle—which will remain hidden in the cab of my truck.

I mean, it's not like I can let her see it.

Anything with ARMY printed on it goes in the very back of the closet. That includes my PT gear and my Class A uniform, which I'm required to wear to labs on Wednesday and Thursday. I've only worn it twice so far, which would explain why Steph's never seen it. I have no idea how I'm going to get out of the apartment on Wednesday.

Maybe it needs to stay in the cab of the truck, too.

Before I can get too disgusted with myself, I finish unpacking my clothes. I have no pictures, so there's nothing to hang on the walls. My books now have a home on the nightstand, and my laptop is charging on top of the small dresser.

I save the best for last.

The bed.

Tessa, the sweet girl she is, left me everything—the sheets, the pillows, even the comforter. She could have stripped it bare and I wouldn't have cared.

With a contented sigh, I lay down on the mattress. My feet don't dangle. I can turn. I can twist. I can flop. And when I do, all six-foot-two-inches of me remains *on the bed.*

Unbelievably—or maybe not considering how comfortable I am— I fall asleep, and I don't wake up until I hear Steph's voice behind the door, calling my name.

It's the only thing that could get me out of that bed. After taking another good look around to make sure everything that needs to be hidden is out of sight, I open the door.

"Hey, roomie."

"Hey. All settled?" she asks, taking a peek inside.

"Yep. It didn't take long. I even took a nap."

"Well, I brought pizza. You're welcome to share."

"Okay."

I follow her to the kitchen, which smells like heaven thanks to the large pepperoni and sausage waiting for us on the table.

"How was class?" I ask as we take our seats.

"Terrible. I hate Physics."

"Why?"

She reaches for a slice. "It's just a lot of math. That's why I'm an English major, so that I can avoid teaching anything that remotely involves numbers."

"I'm okay at math, but I like science. Taking things apart. Putting them back together. Making them work when no one else can."

"Like computers?"

"Computers, radio and satellite systems . . . anything that can be programmed, really."

"Do you have a job waiting for you in Georgia?"

I choke on my pizza. *How does she know about Georgia?* Steph offers me a bottle of water, which I accept gratefully and guzzle down. As I do, I pray for an answer—an answer that doesn't require me to lie.

"Better?"

I clear my throat. "Yeah, thanks."

"Good." Steph offers me a napkin. "So, what's in Georgia?"

"How do you know about Georgia?"

"You told us at dinner, remember? The night Tessa cooked you a Mexican buffet?"

Oh yeah.

"I just have some additional training. It's required." Relieved that I managed to give her a vague version of the truth, I quickly change the subject. "You know, I could probably help you with your Physics. What was tonight's lesson?"

"I have no idea. It was completely over my head, so I spent the entire time coming up with a list of rules."

"Rules?"

"For us." Steph wipes her hands on a napkin before reaching into her backpack. She pulls out a sheet of notebook paper and hands it to me. Sure enough, right at the top, *THE RULES* is written in black ink.

"You actually made a list?"

She nods. "I'm a big believer in lists."

With a chuckle, I scan the page. My laughter quickly fades when I read the first rule on the page.

#1. No touching.

"Seriously, Steph? We're not allowed to touch each other?"

"Not in the apartment, no."

"Is kissing considered touching?"

"Keep reading."

#2. No kissing.

What a bunch of crap.

"This is honestly what you want?"

"I never said it's what I want. I just think we have to keep a respectable distance when we're in the apartment. If we're on a date, the rules don't exist. But when we're home, I really think we need to try to keep our hands to ourselves."

I try to find the logic in that, but it escapes me, so I keep reading. The rest of the list is just basic roommate info. Rent is due on the first of the month. Utilities on the fifteenth. I take out the trash; she cleans the bathroom. Evenly divided responsibilities, right down to who cleans the litter box.

"That's mine," Steph says simply. "She's my cat, so . . ."

I nod. Bangle hates me, anyway.

"Is the list okay?"

I shrug. "I'm fine with everything—except for numbers one and two. From what I can recall, we *like* touching each other. I think you're just setting us up for failure."

"I'd like to try anyway."

"But dating is okay?"

"Yes."

"And we can kiss on dates, but not in the apartment."

"Right."

"Why does it matter?"

Steph sighs and pushes away her empty plate. "I just think we will . . . behave ourselves if we're out in public."

Translation: There are no soft, comfy beds out in public.

"Steph, I promised to be respectful, and I will be."

"I know you did. But like I said, I may not *want* you to be. Maybe having established rules will keep us from tempting fate."

She's giving this sheet of paper a lot of power. I hope it works.

Remember, Brandon. Let her lead.

"Okay. Where's a pen?"

She finds one in her backpack, and we both sign at the bottom. If this is what it will take to get her to trust me, I'll write my name on whatever she wants.

In an unspoken attempt to follow the stupid rules, we occupy ourselves and our hands with homework. I don't know if it's a conscious decision, but we both end up on the couch. I'm on one side, she's on the other, and in the middle is her evil cat.

Staring at me.

Steph pretends to read from an ancient paperback copy of *The Silence of the Lambs* while I pretend to study a chapter on operating systems. Her eyes might be glued to the page, but she's not fooling me. She has a little smile on her face, and I know for a fact there's not a thing in that book that would give her a warm, fuzzy feeling.

"You know, Brandon, you'd get more accomplished if you looked at your book."

"It's not as pretty."

Sighing softly, Steph shakes her head before turning her attention back to her book. I can see the faint blush of her cheeks, and I watch in fascination as it spreads down her neck. My hand twitches in response, which leads Bangle to hiss in my direction.

Stupid cat.

I realize I'm being distracting, which was her fear all along, so I decide to give it up and call it a night.

"I should try to sleep. I have to be up at five."

Steph closes her book. "You always get up at five?"

"Yep."

"To work out?"

I nod. "Only three days are required, but I do six."

"I've never understood why an engineering major has required workouts."

Shit.

"It's umm . . . for an elective PE course I'm taking."

It's not exactly a lie, but it still leaves a bad taste in my mouth.

We stand and walk down the hallway toward our bedrooms. Our *adjacent* bedrooms—you know, because just being under the same roof isn't temptation enough. The bell on Bangle's collar jingles, letting us know that she's hot on our heels. When Steph opens her bedroom door, the feline gives me one last hiss before heading inside.

Steph smirks. "See? You're growing on her."

"Yeah, like a fungus."

We both laugh and lean a little closer. The urge to touch her is overwhelming. The need to kiss her is worse.

"You're driving me crazy, Steph."

"I don't mean to."

"You can't help it."

She smiles.

"Sleep well, Brandon."

"You, too."

And I do. It's my best night's sleep since the semester began.

When I wake up the next morning, I quietly climb out of bed and make my way to the shower. I know Steph's first class isn't until ten, so I don't want to wake her any earlier than necessary. As I stumble into the bathroom, I flip on the light, and there on the mirror is a yellow sticky note. I wipe the sleep from my eyes, and when I'm able to finally focus on the words, I can't help but grin.

Brandon,

You drive me crazy, too.

Love,

Steph

By the end of January, Steph and I fall into a comfortable, if not frustrating, routine. I'm out of the house each morning by five, and I don't usually see her again until later that night. Between my PT, weekend field experience, regular classes, and my job at The Grind, combined with her six classes and her job at the library, we've barely had time to say hello. We had planned a couple of movie nights, but something always happened to screw it up. My PT would run late, or she'd have a last-minute project that had to be completed. Or Xavier and Tessa would stop by. The only time we're really together—and awake—is during Women's lit, and we can't do anything in there except hold hands.

I just want to kiss her . . . for an extended period of time. *Is that too much to ask?*

It's Friday afternoon, and The Grind is pretty dead, so I'm using the free time to study. I've just started reading a chapter on military ethics when I hear my sister's ringtone.

"Sister Christian." I bet Steph loves that song.

"Hey, Chris."

"Don't *hey* me. You hung up on me and didn't call back."

"Yeah, well, I wasn't in the mood for a lecture, and I'm still not, so unless you're calling to talk about Dad or the girls—"

"It's about Dad."

This shuts me up, and I listen as Christian tells me that she's had to take over Dad's personal finances after the bank informed her that he had overdrawn on his checking account.

"And it wasn't a small amount," Christian explains. "We're talking thousands of dollars. He's been a customer for decades so they've been really understanding, and he had savings to cover it, but I've basically had to hide his wallet and checkbook."

Bruce Walker is a decorated war hero and deacon in the church. He survived two tours in Vietnam and a divorce after thirty years of marriage. Our dad is respected in the community and stubborn as a mule. I can only imagine how deeply it's wounded his pride to have his daughter take over his finances.

Alzheimer's sucks. And this is supposedly the *early* stages.

I try to swallow the lump in my throat. "I should be there."

"No, you should be right where you are. You have an obligation, Brandon. The United States Army owns you for the next four years."

"I know, Chris."

"That's why I said it was terrible that you like that girl," she says. "Don't get me wrong. It's great that you've met someone, and if you can keep it casual, and keep it in your pants—"

"I am *not* having this conversation with you."

She takes a deep breath. "You're headed to Fort Gordon in June. After that, who knows where you'll be. A serious girlfriend—whether she likes the military or not—is not a good idea. Not right now. You need to stay focused on school and your field exercises. Fulfill your duty. Serve your country. You have all the time in the world to fall in love."

I chuckle. "I'm not in—"

"Maybe not. Not yet. But when my brother calls me and starts talking about some girl's big brown eyes and her sweet laugh, I know it's just a matter of time. And I bet he does, too. That's why the very best thing you can do for yourself and for . . . what's her name again?"

"Stephanie. Steph."

"The best thing you can do for yourself and Steph is forget that she exists. You'll just break her heart, and doing that will break yours. You need to stay away from her. For both your sakes."

Probably not the best time to talk about the new roommate.

"You're right, Chris. I know you are."

"Good."

We hang up, and I spend the rest of my shift in misery. Deep down, I know Christian's right. Even if Steph didn't despise the military, we'd still be doomed. What kind of future can I offer her when I don't even know where I'm going to be for the next four years?

And why are you even considering a future with a girl you've barely known for a month?

I'm still pondering that question when one of our regular customers walks into the shop. Sylvia Metcalf is seventy-two and loves onion bagels with her French roast coffee. She's a widow and has a granddaughter named Amber who is around my age. I know this because she tells me *every single time* she sees me.

"How are you today, Mrs. Metcalf?"

"Oh, can't complain," Mrs. Metcalf replies, but she proceeds to do exactly that. The weather sucks, her back hurts, and the snow tires on her Buick need replaced.

"You look preoccupied today," she says as I ring her up. "Something on your mind?"

"A few things, actually. School. Family."

"You know, a girl could take your mind right off those troubles," she says, with a twinkle in her eye. "That's all you need. A sweet girl. I have a granddaughter . . ."

My chest tightens as I think about the only girl I want to see. The only girl that matters.

I look down at my watch. "You know what, Mrs. Metcalf? I think you're right."

She brightens. "I am?"

I hand her the bagel and coffee.

"Yep. A sweet girl is just what I need. And I know exactly where to find her."

chapter
nine

Stephanie

"So the pharmacology books are in the 600s?"

"615, yes."

The nursing student looks confused as she glances at the bookshelf. "But this sign says the 600s are Technology."

"That's right."

"Shouldn't it be in the 500s? In Sciences?"

God, give me patience.

My entire afternoon in the library has been just like this, with one annoying question right after the other. Where's this book? Where's that book? How much is my overdue fine? Do you have a vending machine? Can I check out a laptop? Ms. Maria, the librarian, even threatened to send me home early if I didn't chill out. Now, I have this little blonde nursing student with a ridiculous interest in the Dewey Decimal System, and I am just *not* in the mood.

"This way." I lead her toward the appropriate shelf and point at the large volume titled *Side Effects: The Big Book of Pharmacology*. "Is this the book you need?"

"Yes, but . . ."

I hand it to her. "This book is classified as *Medical* science, and books related to medicine are in the Technology category."

"But *why* is it in Technol—"

"I don't know why! I don't care why! I wasn't alive back in the 1870s when Mr. Dewey developed his system! Now, please, for the love of God, just take the book and go."

The girl frowns. "You need a mood stabilizing drug. Maybe something with a mild antidepressant."

"I need a lot of things. Have a nice day."

The girl rolls her eyes at me before heading to the checkout counter.

Taking a deep breath, I lean my forehead against the spines of the medical books. *What is wrong with me?* Yes, I'm tired. Yes, I'm stressed. But I've never been rude to other students, especially when I'm on the clock. I just feel . . . off. Grouchy. Frustrated.

Suddenly, I feel a pair of hands on my waist.

"I know what you need," he whispers in my ear.

With those words, and with that voice, every ounce of tension leaves my body. I turn around, and Brandon steps closer, pinning me between his body and the shelf.

"Hi." My voice is soft and whispery and *so* not me.

"Hey." He plays with a strand of my hair. "Rough day?"

"Rough week. *Weeks*."

"Mine, too. I've missed you."

And that's when I realize the reason behind my foul mood. *Could it really be that simple?*

"I've missed you, too."

"Better now?"

"Getting there."

With a grin, he lowers his head, and I sigh softly as his lips trail along my neck. I wrap my arm around him and pull him harder against me, making him groan. This section of the library stays pretty deserted, but it's still a little too out in the open for this level of PDA.

However . . .

"Come with me," I tell him.

Pulling him by the hand, I lead him through the labyrinth of shelves until we reach the periodical closet. The room is filled with outdated catalogs and is rarely used.

It also locks, and I have a key.

We step inside. As soon as the lock clicks into place, Brandon lifts me into his arms and spins around, pinning me against another shelf. I wrap my legs around his waist just as his lips crash into mine. Warm. Wet. Frantic. I grip his shoulders as he holds me tight against his body, and for the first time, I can feel just how much he wants me.

Overwhelmed by the intensity of the moment, I bury my face against his neck and cling to him. He hugs me close, whispering my name and telling me how much he missed me.

Over the past few weeks, we've been like ships passing in the night. He gets up at five; I'm a night owl. Neither of us understood how hectic our schedules really were until we tried to carve some time out to just *see* each other.

"It's Friday. I want to see you tonight," he says softly, lowering me onto the floor. "I don't care what it takes. Let me take you somewhere."

"We don't have to go anywhere. We can just stay home."

"I can't kiss you at home."

Me and my stupid rules.

"I have to kiss you, Steph."

He proves it by kissing me again. This time, it's slow and sweet. He kisses my lips, my cheeks, my eyelids . . . anywhere his mouth can easily reach.

I sigh softly. "We could . . . go to the movies."

"We could. What should we watch?"

"Doesn't matter."

He can drag me to a bloody slasher flick for all I care. Just the fact that we will be within touching distance for at least two hours tonight is enough.

After a few more kisses, we quietly sneak out of the periodical closet. Brandon holds my hand until we reach the counter. Ms. Maria watches us with interest as we say goodbye.

He leans close and kisses my forehead. "See you tonight."

Then he's gone, and I'm practically floating as I step behind the counter.

"Well, you seem happier," Ms. Maria says, her voice tinged with just a hint of laughter. "Nothing like a little library lovin' to perk a girl right up, eh?"

My face flames, and she gives me a wink before walking back to her office.

When Brandon asked the girl at the box office for two tickets to the French documentary, I thought he had lost his mind. But now that we're in the darkened theater, with a grand total of four other people, I'm thinking he's a total genius.

"Thirty minutes left," Brandon whispers against my ear.

His mouth finds mine in the darkness, and I try to remember how long the movie lasts. Two hours, maybe? And we haven't looked at the screen once. We're as close as two people can possibly be in the uncomfortable theater seats. Our hands are everywhere, but in true gentlemanly fashion, Brandon has kept his above my clothes and above my waist. Mine, on the other hand, have slipped beneath the fabric of his shirt. His entire body trembles each time my fingers dance across his stomach.

I can't lie. The power makes me a little dizzy.

French dialogue swims in my head as we make out like a couple of teenagers, until finally, the credits roll and the fluorescents flicker to life.

"Meilleur film que j'ai jamais vu," Brandon says.

Holy crap. "You speak French?"

"And Spanish and German."

Brandon buttons his shirt and I try to fix my hair while trying to ignore the knowing looks of the people who walk past on their way to the exit.

"People are staring," I mutter.

"Screw 'em. They're just jealous."

I laugh and loop my arm through his as we head out of the theater. We've just stepped outside when someone yells Brandon's last name. He doesn't turn around. Instead, he quickens his pace, and we've barely made it to his truck when the guys catch up with us.

"Walker! What's your hurry man?"

"Yeah, aren't you going to introduce us to your pretty girlfriend?"

Brandon sighs and turns around. We're greeted by a couple of guys, both dressed in gray hoodies with *Army Strong* printed across the chest.

"Damien. Jon."

Brandon wraps his arm around me and pulls me closer as he makes the introductions. The guys don't really make me feel uncomfortable, but there's something about Brandon's protective stance that makes me think he doesn't really like them too much. His body is rigid; his face is pale.

Damien smiles at me. "So you're the reason Walker is in such a hurry to get home at night."

"Can't say I blame him," Jon says, eyeing me from head to toe. "We're headed to a mixer over at Sigma Chi. You guys should come."

"I don't think so," Brandon says.

Normally, I'd be upset that he didn't even ask if I was interested in going, but in this case, I'm glad. I'm never in the mood for a frat party, and

Brandon acts like he would rather clean Bangle's litter box than spend another minute with these guys.

Brandon opens the passenger-side door and all but shoves me into the cab of the truck before slamming the door. I hear him tell the guys he'll see them on Monday before he climbs in and quickly starts the ignition.

"Friends of yours?"

"Not really."

I buckle my seatbelt as he points the truck toward the highway. Turning toward him, I notice his face still looks panicked. His hands are wrapped tightly around the steering wheel.

"You have classes with them?"

I hear him take a deep breath and exhale slowly. "What makes you think that?"

"Well, Damien said you were in a hurry to get home at night. I figured you had a class with him or something."

Brandon nods stiffly and continues to drive.

"We do have a few classes together," he says quietly.

"But you don't like them."

"I like them fine."

It isn't the answer I'm expecting at all. Something is obviously wrong.

"Are you mad about the party? Because we can go."

He frowns. "Do you want to go?"

"Not really, but I'll go if you want."

Brandon shakes his head and veers to the right, stopping abruptly on the shoulder of the road. He throws off his seatbelt before reaching for mine, and within seconds, he's pulling me sideways into his lap. I don't care that I'm pinned between him and the steering wheel as he holds me close. This is my happy place. My favorite place.

"I just wanna be with you, Steph. I don't care where we are."

He weaves his hands into my hair and pulls my face close. His brown eyes look pained, and I wish I knew why.

"Tell me what's wrong," I whisper against his lips.

He just shakes his head and kisses me, lightly at first, but his lips grow urgent until we're swallowing each other's moans. This kiss isn't like the playfulness in the theater. There's desperation here, a frantic fear that I wish I understood.

But I don't.

Brandon buries his head against my shoulder. I slide my fingers along his scalp, and it's moments like this when I wish he didn't have such short hair.

"Thank you for tonight, Brandon."

He lifts his head and smiles softly. "Thank you for tonight, too."

I kiss him gently before climbing back to my side of the truck.

The drive home is a quiet one, but this time, he holds my hand as he drives. He doesn't let go until we reach our apartment building.

"Wait here," he says.

I smile as he climbs out of the truck and walks around to my door. He opens it and offers me his hand. I'm short, so climbing in and out of his truck is a pain, but I know that's not why he does it. He helps me out of the truck and offers me his arm as we walk to the apartment door because he's a gentleman. I'd almost forgotten what one looked like. But mine is handsome, with close-cropped strawberry blonde hair and big brown eyes.

And he speaks French.

"What did you say?" I ask once we're inside the apartment. "Back at the movies, when you wowed me with your French accent? What did you say?"

"Meilleur film que j'ai jamais vu," he says. "Best movie ever."

I grin. "It really was."

Brandon takes a step closer and lifts his palm toward my face. Suddenly, he shakes his head and quickly stuffs his hand into his pocket.

"Stupid rules," I mutter.

"I'm happy to rip them to shreds at any time. Just say the word."

So tempting.

"That would be dangerous, Brandon."

He sighs before nodding in agreement. "It probably would be. I'm gonna go shower and get some sleep."

"Okay. Will I see you tomorrow?"

"I'll be home after my run. I have a paper to write, so I'll be home all day working on that."

"I need to study, too."

"Meet you on the couch?"

"It's a date."

He turns toward his bedroom. "Goodnight, Steph."

"Goodnight."

chapter Ten

Brandon

The ball flies from my fingertips, bouncing off the backboard and through the net. It's impressive, considering my lack of sleep and the fact that I haven't shot a basketball in months.

Saturdays are my favorite day of the week, and my Saturday morning workouts are typically the best because I don't have to worry about heading to class once they're over. Just a quick run around campus and maybe some conditioning drills before heading to the shower. The rest of the day is for homework or a shift at the coffee shop.

Today's workout sucked. My running time was terrible, and because I had tossed and turned all night, I didn't have the energy to do more than forty-six sit-ups.

Fifty is the *minimum*.

Needless to say, my instructor isn't happy.

Disgusted with myself, I give the basketball a hard bounce, letting it slap against the asphalt. The sound echoes throughout the empty park.

Of course it's empty. Only an idiot would be shooting hoops with snow clinging to the trees.

Xavier had thought I was crazy when I sent him a text, asking him to meet me at the park at nine on a cold Saturday morning. Maybe I am a little insane, but I need to talk, and I need to talk to a guy.

It's times like these when I really miss Vince. We've been best friends since freshman year, but he's now in aviation training at Fort Rucker in Alabama. He doesn't have time to listen to me gripe about the web of lies I've weaved for myself.

Last night was a close call. Too close. I couldn't sleep for thinking how easily I could have lost her.

And make no mistake, I would have lost her.

The ball bouncing on the asphalt covers my bitter laughter. I had been so worried about getting caught in my uniform or my PT gear, but Steph and I had seen so little of each other over the past few weeks that hiding the fact I'm a soldier had been no problem at all.

Until last night.

"Oh, look. Icicles are literally hanging from the backboard."

I grin at Xavier as he makes his way onto the court.

"Seriously, Brandon, it's like twenty degrees."

"The court's clear, though."

"You're still insane."

"No argument here."

He bounces on his toes to stay warm. "And it's Saturday morning. I only wake up this early on a Saturday morning for one person, and she's way hotter than you. She also cooks kickass strawberry waffles. I'm giving up waffles for you, man."

I toss him the ball. "I owe you."

We shoot for over an hour. Xavier is six-foot-seven and a power forward. I'm six-foot-two and sleep-deprived. Keeping score would be embarrassing, so we just play until our fingers are completely frozen.

Xavier grabs the rebound after one of my more humiliating shots. "So, should we just keep freezing our asses off, or are you ready to talk?"

I've stalled long enough.

"I'm ready. Let me buy you a cup of coffee."

We leave his car at the park, and I drive us over to The Grind. After ordering hot chocolates and doughnuts, the two of us find a booth in the corner of the shop.

"I know glazed doughnuts can't compare to Tessa's waffles—"

"*Strawberry* waffles."

"I have a feeling you're gonna be eating strawberry waffles for the rest of your life. Still, I appreciate the sacrifice."

Xavier laughs and takes a bite of his doughnut.

Here goes nothing.

"I need your advice. It's about Steph."

"I assumed."

"I really care about her, Xavier. Probably more than I should. I mean, we haven't really known each other that long."

"I don't think that matters," he replies. "I knew I was in love with Tessa after our first date."

"I'm not in—"

"Oh, whatever. I've seen the way you look at her."

"How do I look at her?"

"Like you're crazy about her."

Am I really that obvious?

"Trust me, Brandon. You suck at hiding it."

Apparently so.

"Steph's never dated much, so the fact that she's so into you has made my girlfriend a very happy woman."

This information makes me smile like a lunatic.

"You think she's into me?"

Xavier chuckles, rolls his eyes, and reaches for another doughnut. "So, what kind of advice do you need?"

I take a deep breath. "I hate to ask, but if I tell you this, can you keep it to yourself?"

"You mean can I keep it from Tessa?"

I nod.

"Brandon, I won't lie to my girl."

"I'm not asking you to lie. Just . . . keep your mouth shut. At least until I can figure out what to do. Because right now, I'm screwed. I just need to know *how* screwed and if there's anything I can do about it. I need your help."

He looks hesitant, and I can't blame him. I know I'm asking a lot. But until I'm sure that he and Tessa will be on my side, I can't trust her with this kind of information. She might tell Steph, and that could ruin everything.

"All right, I'll keep quiet. Let's hear it."

I don't say a word. I simply lower the zipper on my hoodie, revealing my Army ROTC T-shirt.

I hold my breath.

"It's a shirt. I don't get the significance."

"Read it, Xavier."

"I read it. You're in ROTC?"

"Yes."

"That's cool. After that day in the gym, I told Tessa you were way too athletic to be a computer geek. 'Brandon wouldn't lie about something like that,' she said."

"I didn't lie. My major is computer engineering."

"But you're in ROTC?"

"You can do both."

"Huh."

Xavier reaches for another doughnut, but before he can take a bite, a flicker of understanding flashes in his eyes.

His voice drops to a whisper. "Dude . . ."

"I know."

"You're a *soldier*?"

"Don't say it like that. It's not a curse word."

"It is according to Steph's dictionary. That girl has a seriously irrational hatred for the military."

"I know."

"The girls even called you G.I. Joe after that New Year's Eve party. They have no idea how accurate that description turned out to be."

Xavier laughs, and I let him. I need his help, after all, so it's probably best to let him get it all out of his system.

"You're right, man. You're screwed."

"How screwed?"

His laughter fades when he notices the tone of my voice.

"Not sure. I'll need to get a second opinion."

"You mean Tessa."

Xavier nods. "She really likes you. Luckily, she thinks Steph's hatred for anything military related is ridiculous, too."

"That's good, but will she tell Steph?"

"No. I'll talk to her. She'll want to help, and believe me, you're gonna need it."

I make plans to meet up with him and Tessa later in the afternoon, and I drive him back to the park. As I make my way to the apartment, I can't help but feel a little relieved. That went better than I'd hoped.

Now if only my conversation with Tessa goes that well.

After checking that my PT gear is well hidden in the cab, I hit the key fob and head into the apartment. I step inside, and I'm instantly met with the aroma of . . . *charcoal*?

"Steph?"

Suddenly, the smoke alarm blares, and I race toward the kitchen. I find her kneeling in front of the oven, fanning thick, black smoke with a towel.

"It's supposed to be a breakfast casserole . . . thing," she mutters. "I thought the directions said 425 degrees, but apparently not because *look at it!*"

She's close to tears, so the first thing I do is open the nearest window and place the blackened dish on the ledge. Next, I find the irritating fire alarm, pop it open, and rip out the battery. When I walk back into the smoky kitchen, I find Steph sitting at the table, looking forlornly at the oven.

Her eyes find mine. "Tessa makes it look so easy."

I smile and kneel in front of her.

"I bet even the great Chef Tessa burned her fair share of dishes when she was learning how to cook."

She sniffles quietly. "I just wanted to try. I knew you'd be hungry after your workout."

"You baked for me?"

"No, I scorched a big pan of eggs, potatoes, sausage, and cheese . . . for you."

Reaching for her hand, I give it a little squeeze. I know I'm breaking the rules, but I have to touch her. It's impossible not to.

"That was really nice of you, Steph."

"I burned it."

"Doesn't matter."

"And this place smells like smoke."

"But there's a silver lining."

"Which is?"

"At least we don't have a sprinkler system. Although, I must say, seeing you in a wet T-shirt would have made this the *best* Saturday in the history of the world."

This makes her giggle.

"I wish I could make you laugh like that all the time."

She sighs softly, and I'm just about to stand when she leans closer to me. Before I can get too excited, Steph lowers her head and kisses my cheek.

"The rules are so stupid," she whispers in my ear. "But they're smart, too, because you're so sweet, and you say the sweetest things. And when you do, it makes me want . . ."

Her voice trails off, and it's all I can do not to pull her into my arms.

"What do you want, Steph?"

Her cell's ringtone shatters the potentially perfect moment, and she offers me a sad smile before looking down at the screen.

"It's my mom."

I nod. "Go on. I'll get this cleaned up."

"Thank you."

Steph kisses my cheek again before heading to her room.

Now that the smoke has finally cleared, I close the window and try to do something with the charred remains of breakfast. As I stand at the sink, Bangle suddenly appears, and she greets me with a low meow before circling my legs.

"Steph cooked for me, *and* you're wrapping yourself around my ankles? Definitely the best Saturday ever."

Xavier and Tessa's apartment building is like something out of a movie. A doorman greets you at the entrance as you step inside the lobby. The marbled floor shines so brightly you can actually see your reflection, and a man waits inside the elevator just to press the button for you.

How can college kids afford this place?

I knock on 3C, and the door swings open. Tessa immediately pulls me in for a bone-crushing hug. It's impressive, considering she's maybe a hundred pounds soaking wet.

"She's a little excited to see you," Xavier offers in apology.

"Come sit," Tessa says, pulling me by the hand toward the living room. "Are you hungry? We have some leftovers from lunch."

I think about Steph's failed breakfast attempt. It still makes me smile.

"No, thanks. I'm good."

I take a look around at their apartment. There's leather furniture, a large plasma screen, and artwork on the walls.

"Wow, this place is—"

"Ridiculous," Tessa mutters.

"I was going to say *awesome.*"

Xavier shakes his head. "No, she's right. It's ridiculous. My folks own the building. Two college seniors should *not* live in this apartment. I can't even invite my friends over because I'm afraid they'll break something. But the rent is free—"

"And the kitchen is state-of-the-art," Tessa says. "Plus, our parents are letting us live together, so . . ."

"Hey, I understand. I wouldn't turn it down, either."

Xavier wraps his arm around her shoulder, and the room grows quiet.

"So," Tessa says, "Xavier says you want to talk about my beautiful best friend. What's going on?"

I glance at him. "You didn't tell her?"

"I told you I wouldn't."

Sweet.

I clear my throat. "Tessa, I need to tell you something. Something about me."

She sighs and looks between the two of us. "Is this going to piss me off?"

"I don't know. That's why I'm here."

Fire flashes in her eyes. "Are you *married*?"

"What? No!"

She jumps to her feet. "Are you seeing someone else? Because I swear if you break her heart—"

"There's nobody else, Tessa. And I promise the last thing I want to do is break her heart."

I'm suddenly wishing Xavier had just told her already.

Be a man, Walker.

Taking a deep breath, I look Tessa right in the eyes.

"I'm in ROTC. In May, I will graduate as an officer in the United States Army. Then I'm off to Signal Corps training in Fort Gordon, Georgia. After that, I have no idea where I'll be."

The room is suddenly filled with an eerie silence. I don't dare take my eyes off Tessa. I need her, probably more than I've ever needed anybody, because I know her opinion will matter most of all.

"You're a soldier," she whispers.

"Yes."

With wide eyes, she slowly sits back down.

"Oh, Brandon. Why couldn't you be married?"

"That would be *better*?"

"No, but it would be easier to explain."

I tiredly rub my face. *Is she serious?*

"This is bad," Tessa says with a sigh, "but not for the reasons you think. Well, not *entirely* for the reasons you think."

"I don't understand."

"Have you told her you're in the military?"

"Are you nuts?"

"So you're lying to her."

"I am not lying. Not once has Steph asked me if I'm a soldier."

Tessa smirks. "Really? *That's* your defense?"

"It's all I've got."

"It's not enough, Brandon. How could you keep this from her?"

"I didn't know it was something I *needed* to keep from her. I had no idea she felt this way, and by the time I did find out—"

"That was going to be my next question," she says. "When did you find out?"

I grimace. This isn't going to help my case at all.

"The night we watched *The Princess Bride*," I mutter.

"Wasn't that your first official date?"

I nod.

Xavier groans. "Dude—"

"I know, okay? But she had just started opening up to me, and I thought that, with time, she'd come to trust me."

"Which she has," Tessa says softly.

"I know. And I thought that if we lived under the same roof, she'd see that I'm not a bad guy, in spite of the fact that I'm in the Army."

"And then what?" Tessa asks.

"I . . . don't know. I didn't think that far ahead."

"Of course you didn't! You're a guy. Guys don't think ahead. There is only one thing on your minds."

Xavier blinks rapidly. "Hey!"

"Don't *hey* me. Think back to the day we met. Did you really think we'd end up *here* two years later? In this beautifully ridiculous apartment?"

"No, I was just hoping we'd end up in bed." Xavier's mouth snaps closed. "Oh."

Tessa smirks.

"I promise that wasn't my intention when I asked to be her roommate," I tell them. "I've been nothing but a gentleman. You can ask her."

"Oh, I have," Tessa says with a grin. "How are those no-touching rules working for ya?"

"They suck."

Xavier chuckles.

"But if that's what it takes, I'll do it."

Tessa tilts her head, scrutinizing my face with her penetrating stare.

"Why, Brandon? Why do it?"

"Because I'm pretty sure I'm falling in love with her."

The words are out before I can stop them, but I don't care. They need to know I'm serious about this. About her.

Tessa smiles. "And that's wonderful. It really is. Steph is amazing, and she deserves an amazing person who loves her. But she is seriously scarred from the loss of her father. And while it's irrational and, in my opinion, a little immature, that's how she feels and there's really nothing we can do about it."

"I know."

"There's a very good chance she'll hate you for keeping this from her."

"I know that, too."

"And what about you?" she continues. "Are you prepared to have *your* heart broken if Steph doesn't want anything to do with you after she finds out?"

I consider this, and I know that I honestly don't have a choice.

"It's a chance I'm willing to take."

Tessa nods. "Then we'll help you. But you have to find a way to tell her. The only thing that could be worse than Steph finding out you're a solider is if she finds out from somebody else."

I know she's right, and as the two of them walk me to the door, I promise to figure out a way.

"Is it too much to hope for that she could love me . . . in spite of it?"

With a sad smile on her face, Tessa hugs me tightly.

"It could be," she says. "It really could."

chapter
eleven

Stephanie

February 1.

Today's date hits me like a ton of bricks. One minute, I'm rinsing the shampoo out of my hair, and the next, I'm sitting in the tub, letting the roar of the water disguise my quiet sobs.

Today is the anniversary of my dad's death.

Mom even mentioned it last week when she called, but we had talked about it in the abstract, like "your dad's anniversary is coming up." It didn't even dawn on me that it was this weekend. My life really is just too crazy with school and work.

And Brandon.

After drying my hair, I head to my bedroom to finish getting dressed. I look in the mirror and slip my dad's dog tags over my head, but I don't hide them beneath my shirt. Not today. On February 1, the silver metal proudly dangles from my neck for the whole world to see.

I head to the living room and find Brandon on the couch, working on homework. He takes one look at me and frowns.

"What's wrong?"

"I'm a bad daughter."

"I guarantee that's not true."

I join him on the couch. Bangle, sensing my sadness, leaps into my lap. She snuggles close, and I slide my fingers through her fur.

"Today's the anniversary of my dad's death."

Brandon closes his textbook and reaches for my hand. Bangle doesn't even hiss.

Progress.

"I'm sorry, Steph. I didn't know."

"I didn't forget. I never *forget*. The date just . . . caught me by surprise."

"Time gets away from me, too. It's because we're so busy with school."

I nod.

"Do you usually do anything special on this day?"

"Well, if I can get away from school, Mom and I usually visit his grave."

"It's Sunday. We could go."

"You don't have to go, Brandon."

"I know, and if you'd rather just be with your mom, that's completely understandable. I just want you to know that I'm willing to go with you, if you'd like." He grows thoughtful. "Does your mom even know about me?"

"She knows. I can't keep secrets from my mom."

Brandon nods.

"Are you really ready to meet her?"

"I would love that."

"She'll probably cook."

"Even better."

"You're sure?"

"Absolutely. But only if you want me there."

I squeeze his hand, which is a clear violation of the no-touching rule. We've been breaking that rule a lot lately.

"I want you there."

He smiles.

Thanks to sleet and ice on I-70, the drive takes an hour longer than usual. Brandon's a great driver. It's the other idiots on the road that cause him to curse every half-mile or so. By the time we reach the house, the sleet has changed to a soft rain.

Crazy Indiana weather.

Brandon turns off the ignition and looks toward the house. "You ready?"

I nod, and we climb out of the truck. As we step onto the porch, Brandon takes my hand.

"Nervous about meeting my mom?"

"Nope. I just like touching you."

We grin at each other just as the door swings open.

"You're here!" Mom pulls me into her arms, giving me a tight hug that nearly takes my breath away. She's always a little excited when I come home. "I was getting worried. I've heard the interstate is terrible."

"Traffic was crazy. The snow and sleet didn't help. Brandon's a good driver, though."

I step aside, and Mom's gaze immediately locks on him.

"So this is Brandon," she says.

"Yes, ma'am. It's nice to meet you, Mrs. James."

He offers his hand, and I hear my forty-two-year-old mother sigh dreamily before pulling him in for a hug.

I might be a senior in college, but that mattered very little to my mother when I told her my new roommate was a guy. At first, she had the normal fears that any mother would have when you find out that your daughter is living with a strange man. But when I told her I liked him, and that Tessa approved, Mom suddenly had a change of heart. You would think that information would have made a mother even more nervous about the living arrangements, but not mine. She was beyond excited that I was actually interested in someone.

Mom's priorities are seriously out of whack.

"Are you hungry? I made chili. Something warm for a cold day."

She leads us into the kitchen, talking nonstop about the crappy weather. I gather bowls and silverware and place them in the middle of the little round table. There are four chairs, which is two more than we had ever needed.

Until today, that is.

Brandon and I automatically sit next to each other, which makes my mother smile. Throughout lunch, she and Brandon talk about everything—his family, our hometown, even politics and religion. Brandon is his usual charming self, saying all the right things and laughing at Mom's crazy stories.

I sit back and watch it all in fascination. If I had just met him, I would totally think he was full of it.

Can anyone really be this perfect?

Every day, I'm given yet another example of how completely perfect he is, and it scares the crap out of me. Guys, especially twenty-two year olds, are notorious for being jerks that are only after one thing. And while I know Brandon is attracted to me and probably wouldn't turn me down if I wanted to . . . take our relationship to the next level, not once has he been anything short of a gentleman.

Except for that day in the library closet. But I dragged him there.

"What are you smiling about?" Brandon asks.

Crap.

I clear my throat. "Just listening to the two of you."

Mom pours more milk into Brandon's glass. "You're quiet, Stephanie."

"Well, it's hard to get a word in edgewise."

Brandon reaches for my hand. It should be weird holding hands in front of my mom, but it isn't. And one look at Mom's face assures me she doesn't find it weird at all. The woman is practically beaming.

"Stephanie has always been a quiet one. Always thinking. Sometimes, she thinks too much. Worries too much. Doesn't trust herself. I've always told her a little faith is all she needs."

Our eyes lock, and I know she knows I'm having a mental meltdown. Living with my mom for eighteen years made me an expert at reading between the lines. She's telling me to trust my instincts when it comes to Brandon, which I find hilarious because she's known him for a grand total of thirty minutes.

"You know, *she's* right here," I mumble. "Could we maybe talk about something besides me?"

"That's another thing," Mom says, "She absolutely *hates* attention."

Brandon chuckles. "I've noticed that, actually."

I roll my eyes.

Mom laughs before turning her attention to the window. "I'm worried about you driving back tonight. We've had a rain-snow-sleet mix all day. The roads may freeze tonight. Can you stay the night and drive back tomorrow?"

"I was just thinking about that, actually," Brandon replies, glancing at me. "What do you think?"

"My first class isn't until the afternoon. What about your morning run?"

He shrugs. "I can run anywhere."

"You're a runner?" Mom asks.

"Brandon wakes up at five o'clock every morning to work out."

Mom makes a sour face. "Why?"

"I know, right? He's very regimented. Very disciplined."

Mom hums quietly and smiles at Brandon, making him sigh and shift uncomfortably in his chair.

"*Now* who's hating the attention?"

We all laugh, and Brandon offers to clear the table while Mom and I head to the living room. I follow her over to the sofa.

"I like him, Steph."

I grin. "Really? I couldn't tell."

She suddenly grows serious and reaches for the chain around my neck. Her fingers slide along the metal.

"I'm glad you're here today. Both of you."

"He wasn't sure if he should come."

"But you wanted him here."

"Yeah."

"Is it serious?"

"Not yet, no."

"But it could be?"

I look toward the kitchen. "I think it could be, yeah."

"What's keeping it from being serious?"

"Me."

She nods. "I figured as much. You should trust your instincts, Steph."

"I can't."

"Why not?"

"Because this is completely foreign to me. I can't trust this because I've never experienced it."

"Experienced what?"

"Whatever *this* is."

We're talking in circles now, which isn't unusual for us.

"My instincts tell me he's pretty perfect," I admit quietly. "But how can that be? *Nobody* is."

"Your dad had his perfect moments."

I glance toward the fireplace mantle. That's where Dad's picture has been proudly displayed since before I was born. Rising from the couch, I walk over and stare at the gold frame. He's wearing his uniform, and an American flag is displayed in the background.

"I'm going to help Brandon with the dishes," Mom says quietly, leaving me alone with my dad and my jumbled thoughts.

It never fails to amaze me just how handsome my father was, especially in his uniform. He looked so dignified and proud, leaving no doubt in my mind that he loved the military. But it's impossible for me not to feel sad when I look into his eyes, because all I can think about is how much he's missed. Holidays. Birthdays. Growing old and gray with his wife. He won't see me graduate from college, and he won't get to walk me down the aisle.

Was the military really worth missing all that?

I have no idea how long I stand there, but after a while, I feel Brandon's arms wrap around my waist. He gently pulls me close to his chest and rests his chin on my shoulder.

"You have his eyes," he says.

"Yeah."

He holds me tight in his arms as we stare at the picture of my father.

"The rain has stopped. Cynthia says if we want to go to the cemetery, we should probably go now."

I turn around in his arms. "*Cynthia* says, huh?"

"That's what she told me to call her."

"You are quite the charmer, aren't you?"

Brandon smiles and gently places his hand on my cheek.

"There's only one girl I'm interested in charming."

"Well, mission accomplished."

Brandon lowers his head, kissing me gently.

"You're sure you want me there?"

"I do."

He nods and we grab our coats off the couch just as mom returns to the living room. She adjusts the scarf around her neck and zips her jacket.

"Are we ready?"

Brandon and I nod, and the two of us follow Mom to her car.

The small cemetery rests on a hillside just behind the Methodist church. A dusting of snow covers the grass and ice has settled on the tombstones. The rain has stopped for now, but the wind is bitterly cold. I tighten my scarf around my neck, but my body trembles anyway.

"Are you okay?" Brandon asks.

"Just cold."

He wraps his arm around me as we walk toward the gravesite. Mom is ahead of us, and I don't know if it's because she wants to give us privacy or if she wishes it for herself. Her mood has changed drastically since we left the house, but that's to be expected, I think. And I know, once we return home, we'll probably have something simple for dinner before Mom heads to her bedroom for the night. That's been the routine since I was little, and while I didn't understand it as a young girl, I get it now. She needs her time, too. Time to grieve. Time to remember. I don't expect her routine to change just because we're visiting, and I wouldn't want it to.

A concrete bench rests next to Dad's grave. It's damp and cold, but on this day, Mom always brings a blanket. She lays it across the bench and the three of us sit down, with me in the middle. Brandon takes my hand while I reach for Mom's with the other. She and I never say anything during these visits—at least not out loud—but I silently talk to my dad, telling him about whatever's going on in my life. I suspect Mom does the same, but we don't talk about it.

Today, I have a lot to say.

Hi, Dad. I'm graduating this year. I'm going to be an English teacher, and I can't wait to see my very first classroom. I wish you were here to see it, too. I wish you were here to watch me walk across the stage at graduation. And I wish I wasn't bitter that you aren't. Maybe someday, I won't be. Everyone says I should be proud of your sacrifice, and I guess I am. But I don't understand it. I don't see how the war could have been more important than your marriage. Or me. Maybe someday I'll understand, but today is not that day, and I'm sorry about that.

As if he knows I need the support, Brandon gives my hand a reassuring squeeze.

Dad, this is Brandon. He's really wonderful. I think you'd approve. I know Mom does. I really like him. I think . . . I could love him. I think he could love me, too.

After a while, Mom sighs softly and rises to her feet.

"It's getting colder," she says.

Taking that as our cue, Brandon and I stand up, too.

He glances up at the sky. "Those look like snow clouds to me."

Mom and I turn to go, but Brandon doesn't move. Instead, his eyes are now fixed on my father's grave.

With a solemn expression on his face, Brandon stands ramrod straight and gives the tombstone a salute.

chapter
Twelve

Brandon

Running on a snowy trail is rarely fun, but it's good practice. As a soldier, you obviously have no idea where you might be stationed, so getting used to extreme weather is part of our conditioning drills. Still, running on ice is kind of impossible, so I'm grateful to find that the roads are snow-covered, giving me just enough traction to not kill myself.

The road crews are already out, clearing the snow from the highway. One of the trucks even stopped for me, and the driver asked if I needed a lift. When I told him I was out for my morning run, he looked at me like I was an idiot before moving on.

The sun is just beginning to rise when I turn around and jog back toward the house. My plan is to take a hot shower and then make breakfast for Steph and her mom before we head back to campus.

Yesterday was hard for them. And for me. For the very first time, I actually got a very real glimpse of the sadness that Steph feels every single day. It hit me hard, seeing the grave of her father. Not only did it make me think about my own dad, but it also made me think about my future.

As soldiers, we're taught that putting our lives on the line is our honor. Our duty. It was ingrained in me as a boy and it's being drilled into my head now, but yesterday, I had my very first moment of doubt.

Is this really what I want to do?

I used to think so. Maybe because it was expected of me, or maybe because I just didn't know what else I wanted to do with my life, but being a soldier has always been the plan. It was a no-brainer, committing to four years with the United States Army in exchange for paid college tuition. My dad was thrilled, my sister was satisfied, and there was absolutely nothing (like a girlfriend) standing in my way. Making a career out of it never appealed to me, but I was ready to serve my country and then start living my life. I wanted to find an engineering job, maybe in Lexington or Louisville. Or maybe leave Kentucky altogether and start building a life.

And now, I might actually have someone to spend that life with.

If I've learned anything during this trip, it's that Tessa is right. I have to tell Steph the truth, and I have to do it soon.

I stop at the porch, taking a few minutes to stretch before heading inside. After taking a hot shower and changing into sweats, I head to the kitchen to raid Cynthia's fridge. I stop in my tracks when I find her sitting at the table.

"Good morning, Brandon."

"Good morning," I say, smiling. "I was hoping to surprise you both with breakfast."

"I've always been an early bird." She gets up and walks over to the stove. "I made eggs and bacon. Would you like a plate?"

"Sounds great."

"Coffee?"

"Juice, please, if you have it."

"It's in the fridge. Help yourself."

I find a glass and head to the refrigerator. When I get back to the table, a plate filled with bacon, scrambled eggs, toast, and gravy is waiting for me.

"Thank you, Cynthia."

She smiles, and I dig in.

"How did you sleep? I worried about you on the couch."

"It was pretty comfortable, actually."

"I'm glad. Where did you say you're from?"

It's not unexpected, but I'm still a little surprised with the interrogation. *Couldn't she wait until after breakfast?*

"A little town called Applewood. It's in Eastern Kentucky."

"How was your run?"

"It was cold."

"How was your running time?"

"Decent. Just over fourteen minutes."

"How are the roads?"

"Crews are already out. We should have no problem getting back to campus."

"And when are you going to tell my daughter you're a soldier?"

My fork falls, causing it to clang against the plate. I swallow so quickly the eggs burn my throat.

How does she know? My expression must reflect my panic, because she smiles.

"Relax, Brandon. Your secret's safe with me. For now."

Cynthia pours more juice into my glass, and I gulp it down before clearing my throat.

"How . . . I mean, how . . .?"

"How did I figure it out?" she asks, and I nod. "Your hair, for one. Of course, not everyone who has short, cropped hair is in the military, but it was my first hint. My second clue was the fact that you wake up at five o'clock every single morning. Very few college seniors wake up before dawn to exercise. That takes dedication, discipline, and obligation. But my final clue was at the cemetery."

My forehead creases. *How? I didn't say a word at the cemetery.*

"Not everyone knows the proper stance and technique for a salute. Tip of finger touching the outer edge of the right eyebrow. Thumb in the right place. Your hand and wrist forming a straight line from your elbow to your fingertips. Upper arm horizontal to the ground. Most civilians do it wrong, but when you saluted Billy's grave, it was perfect. Too perfect for someone who doesn't practice it every day."

It should be perfect. I had been taught by the master.

"I wasn't a military wife for long, but it was long enough." she says. "I'm guessing Army. Am I right?"

With a heavy sigh, I push my plate aside.

"Yes."

"ROTC?"

I nod. "After I graduate in May, I'm headed to Signal Corps training for three months."

"And after that?"

"I don't know."

She nods in understanding. Of course she understands.

"I'm assuming Stephanie has no idea."

I shake my head. "I need to tell her soon. I know that."

"Yes, you do. You know, she tells me the two of you aren't serious yet, but I'm not sure I believe her. You're the only boy she's ever dared to bring home, and you're certainly the first she's taken to her father's grave. She wanted you there, which tells me that she trusts you. You don't want that trust shattered by keeping something like this from her for too long."

"She'll hate me . . ." My voice cracks, but I can't hide my fear anymore. More than anything, I'm afraid she'll hate me forever.

With a heavy sigh, Cynthia slides her chair closer and places her hand on top of mine. It's a kind, motherly touch that feels completely foreign but is comforting all the same.

"Stephanie definitely has her opinions about the military. I have spent the better part of twenty-two years trying to make her understand that her father didn't *choose* the Army over his family. I thought perhaps as she got older, she would become more rational, but it's yet to happen."

"She just misses not having a father. I can understand that."

Cynthia nods. "Billy was my high school sweetheart and the love of my life. He made it no secret that he wanted to join the Army, and if you joined in 1990, you were more than likely headed to the Middle East. I begged him to marry me before he left for Basic. My parents tried to convince me to wait, but I wouldn't hear of it. I wanted to be his wife, and Billy would do anything to make me happy, so we were married a few weeks before he went to Fort Benning. After graduation, he came home on leave, and that's when I told him I was pregnant. He was so happy, and I was, too. He was headed to Advanced Individual Training, and we knew I could join him when he finished there. But that all changed when the Gulf War began. He had another short leave and then was sent to Kuwait. He was killed two weeks later."

Her voice breaks, just a little, giving me a glimpse of the emotion she tried so hard to hide from us last night.

"I'm sorry, Cynthia."

"Thank you. It's been more than twenty years, but the heartache never really goes away. My beautiful daughter has his eyes and his stubbornness. And while the latter frustrates me to no end, I wouldn't change her for the world."

"I don't want to change her. I just want to . . ."

"Love her?"

I inhale sharply. "Maybe?"

A door creaks open, and I hold my breath. After a few moments, we hear another door close and the shower roar to life.

I sigh with relief.

"If that's true, then you have to be honest with her," Cynthia says. "Just remember that her reaction—and it probably won't be pretty—will have nothing to do with you *or* the military. It will have everything to do with *me*."

I frown. "With you? I don't understand."

"Brandon, don't you see? My daughter's greatest fear is ending up like me."

The sadness in her voice is palpable, and I wish I had the right words to make it better, but I don't. What she says makes perfect sense. Steph's hatred isn't irrational at all. It's a defense mechanism, engineered to protect her heart.

If you don't let it in, it can't hurt you.

"I'm so screwed," I mutter.

Cynthia laughs quietly and pats my hand. "I don't think so. I think you might just be the incentive my daughter needs to finally remove that bitter chip off her shoulder. Fear and hate will eat at you, Brandon. It can make you cold and distant. It can make you question your instincts and hide your heart. It's time for my daughter to stop hiding. But you have to tell her the truth, and soon."

"I will. I promise."

"That's good." Cynthia smiles. "I like you, Brandon, and I apologize for the motherly interrogation. They probably don't teach that in the military."

"They should. It's effective."

We both laugh just as Steph makes her way into the kitchen. She stops and looks at us as if we've lost our minds.

"You guys are way too happy for this early in the morning."

I chuckle. She is *so* not a morning person.

After breakfast, I offer to clean up so that Steph and her mom can have a few minutes together before we leave. They head to the living room, and while I can see them on the couch, I try not to listen to their conversation. I still hear my name a few times, but I ignore it and focus on loading the dishwasher. Once the kitchen is as clean as I can possibly get it, I slowly make my way into the living room.

"Ready to go?" Steph asks.

"If you are."

"I'll just get my jacket."

Steph disappears down the hallway, and I grab my own coat that's hanging on the hook next to the door. Cynthia follows me out onto the porch.

"Thank you for cleaning, Brandon."

"No problem. Thank you for breakfast . . . and dinner. And the talk."

She pulls me in for a hug, as if it's the most natural thing in the world. Steph appears on the porch and they hug, too. Cynthia makes me promise to drive safely, and we say goodbye before heading down the slushy steps.

Steph is quiet on the way back to campus, and I can't help but wonder what she and her mom talked about just before we left. But I don't ask.

Instead, I try to pinpoint why I have such an empty feeling in my gut.

I feel Steph's eyes on me, but I stay focused on the road. The highway is clear for the most part. Just a few patches of snow and ice here and there. Still, I don't want to lose my concentration for a minute. That's how accidents happen.

"Mom really likes you," Steph says.

"I like her, too. She's sweet. Just like a mom should be."

"Was that hard for you? Meeting her?"

"Not at all. I enjoyed meeting her."

"That's not really what I meant."

I feel it again . . . that little twinge in my stomach that I can't quite figure out.

"My mom can be affectionate," she says. "She's a big hugger. I just wondered if it made you feel uncomfortable. Or sad. You know, because . . ."

Because of my mom.

I consider that. I don't feel *sad*, exactly, but I wonder if Cynthia's motherly affection is the reason I'm feeling . . . whatever it is I'm feeling.

"It's been a long time since I've been hugged by a mom," I admit quietly.

"Was it weird?"

"Not at all. It was nice."

"I'm glad. And I really appreciate you going with me. You didn't have to do that, but I'm grateful you did."

"I'd do anything for you, Steph."

She reaches across the console and laces her fingers with mine. Steph smiles at me with her sweet, trusting eyes, and I know I have to find a way to tell her the truth.

Time to soldier on, even if it means losing her.

chapter

Thirteen

Brandon

Once a month, ROTC students are required to wear fatigues and volunteer at Magnolia Gardens, a local nursing home for veterans. We play checkers, help with crafts, read stories, or just sit and talk. Over the past few semesters, I've gotten especially close to a man by the name of Tom McBride. Tom served two tours in Vietnam and was awarded the Purple Heart after a grenade attack left him completely blind. Despite his disability, Tom went on to graduate from college and became a history teacher. He and his wife never had children, so when she passed away last year—and after he suffered his second heart attack—Tom became a permanent resident at Magnolia Gardens. Tom loved the Army and was deeply devoted to his wife until the day she died.

When I find him today, he's sitting on a wooden bench out on the deck. He's wearing a light jacket and his favorite Hoosiers ball cap.

I place my hand on his shoulder. "Afternoon, Tom. The sun's nice today."

He lifts his face to the sky. "Hello, Brandon. Yes, it is. Unseasonably warm for mid-February. Better enjoy it. I heard someone say we might have thunderstorms tonight. Hard to believe we had snow last week. But of course, that's to be expected. You know what they say about Indiana weather."

"If you don't like the weather, just wait a few minutes. You know, we say the same thing in Kentucky."

"Huh." He slides over, making room on the bench so I can join him. "How's school?"

"Very busy. Between my classes and PT, I'm wiped out."

He nods. "Making good grades?"

"So far."

"Good. Dating any pretty girls?"

I frown. "*One* pretty girl, yeah."

"You don't sound too happy about that."

"I'm happy. It's just complicated, Tom."

"People make it complicated. Love. Honesty. Respect. That's all you need. What's so complicated about that?"

I don't have an answer.

"Want to talk about it?"

With a heavy sigh, I lean back against the bench and gaze out across the lawn where a few residents are taking advantage of the sunshine. Most are in wheelchairs, and I always wonder if it was the military or simply old age that made the chairs a necessity.

"Tom, I'm in love with this girl. She's perfect for me in every single way imaginable, except for one."

"Which one?"

"She despises the military."

He sits up a little straighter, and I worry that I've offended him. Instead, he surprises me by asking, "Does she have a reason to hate it?"

"She never met her father. He was killed in Desert Storm before she was born."

"I see. And because of that, she resents the military and everything it stands for."

"Isn't that crazy?"

Tom shakes his head. "It's human nature, Son. For a long time, my wife wouldn't talk about my time in Vietnam. You see, Connie blamed the war for my blindness. She couldn't be mad at *me*, because she loved me. I bet that's how your girl feels. In her mind, the war took away her father. She can't be mad at him, so she lashes out at the thing that took him away."

That makes sense. It still doesn't help my situation.

"She doesn't know I'm in the Army. I haven't told her."

Tom sighs deeply. "Remember what I said? Love. Honesty. Respect. It's hard to have one without the others. You have to tell her."

"But I could lose her."

Tom reaches for my hand. He finds it and gives it a reassuring pat.

"Love. Honesty. Respect. Trust me, Brandon."

A nurse comes out onto the deck, telling Tom it's nearly time for his meds and his afternoon nap.

"A few more minutes," he says.

The nurse nods and smiles at us before heading back inside.

"Wearing your uniform today?"

Thankful for the change of subject, I sigh with relief and glance down at my camo.

"Yeah. Just fatigues and ID tags."

"Don't say *just* fatigues and ID tags. Be proud of them. It's an honor to serve your country, Brandon. Not everyone can do it. Not all young men and women have the determination and drive."

I don't tell him I'm questioning my determination and drive these days. Instead, I offer to read to him from today's newspaper. He's always interested in the news, especially sports, so I make sure to hit the basketball highlights. After a while, I notice he's grown quiet. I lower the paper to find Tom with his eyes closed and his chin resting against his chest. Panic swells inside me, but then he lets out a deafening snore. Chuckling, I wave to one of the nearby nurses.

"Mr. McBride's out like a light," the nurse says. "You must have a soothing voice."

"Or I'm boring, Take your pick."

She laughs and gently wakes Tom. We say goodbye, and the nurse takes his arm to help him to his room.

I spend the rest of the afternoon helping with some holiday craft that involves making carnations out of tissue paper. That's when I realize February

14th is just a few days away. I have no idea what to give Steph for Valentine's Day.

The truth would be nice.

My stupid conscience is becoming pretty vocal, keeping me up at night and making me an irritable ass during the day. I'm just trying to find the right time. The right place. The right moment.

Call me crazy, but something tells me Valentine's Day isn't the answer.

A clap of thunder jerks me awake, interrupting the first decent night's sleep I've had in weeks. Lightning flickers through my window as rain and wind pound overhead.

Tom was right about the storms.

I've always found something cool about severe weather, especially when tornadoes are involved. Then again, maybe I just find them interesting because we don't get a lot of tornadoes in eastern Kentucky. Living in Indiana, where tornado warnings can be a weekly occurrence depending on which part of the state you're in, has certainly opened my eyes to the damage that can come from even the smallest twister. Last year, when an F-2 hit a small town just outside of Evansville, our class spent a weekend repairing roofs and removing uprooted trees in the community as part of our field training exercises.

After that experience, I had a much deeper respect for Mother Nature's fury.

I climb out of bed and throw on a pair of jeans. I head to the bathroom, but as I step out into the hallway, I notice a flicker of light coming from the living room.

Weird.

I peek around the corner, and that's when I see her. Steph is on the couch, wrapped in a blanket with Bangle in her lap. Candles are lit around the room.

"Steph?"

Her head snaps up.

"Hi."

"What's wrong?"

She doesn't answer, so I slowly walk over to the couch. I don't sit down, though. I wouldn't want to invade her space if she'd rather be alone. I also don't want to be clawed by her evil cat.

"Can I sit?"

Steph nods stiffly, and I know something's wrong.

"Crazy storm, huh? Did it wake you up, too?"

"No, I haven't slept."

"Not at all?"

She shakes her head, and I glance down at my watch.

"Steph, it's three in the morning."

"And it's been storming on and off since midnight."

Really? I actually couldn't remember falling asleep. I was so exhausted after the nursing home, I'd barely undressed before collapsing against my pillow.

Thunder crashes overhead, making both of us jump. Steph exhales a quivering breath and holds her cat a little closer.

"What's with the candles?"

"The power went out about an hour ago," she says, her voice trembling. "Bangle . . . she doesn't like storms. I mean, she's seriously afraid of them. She has been since she was a little . . . kitten. "

"Why didn't . . . *Bangle* wake me? I could have kept the two of you company."

"Cats can't open doors, Brandon."

I hide my grin. She has to be the most stubborn woman I've ever met in my life.

"Well, I'm here now. Do you think Bangle would mind if I sat with her until the storm ends?"

Thunder booms again. This time, Steph jumps into my lap and buries her face against my neck. Finally free, Bangle takes the opportunity to make a mad dash for the bedroom.

"Traitor," Steph mumbles.

I chuckle and wrap the blanket around us. Steph lays her head against my shoulder, and I hold her close as the rain batters the roof.

"I'm in your lap," she says quietly.

"So you are."

"That's probably against the rules."

"Probably."

Regardless, she doesn't move, and I'm not about to make her.

"I've always loved the rain," she says. "Mom's house has a metal roof. It can be so peaceful, as long as it's just rain."

"Metal roofs are the best when it rains. We have one, too. It's just one of the many things I miss about home."

Steph lifts her head and gazes at me thoughtfully. "For someone who misses home, you don't talk about it much. Why is that?"

I don't talk much about a lot of things.

"What do you want to know?"

"Tell me the things you miss."

I ghost my fingers along her spine. "I miss the mountains. I miss the sound of the river and the smell of the pines. I miss my church. It's this little country church buried in the woods. We have a congregation of about thirty people, but it can still get pretty loud. I miss my family. My sister needs her brother, and my nieces need their uncle, and I'm not there. And I really miss my dad."

I don't tell her that missing my father is nothing new. I've missed my dad for the past three years. She wouldn't understand, and I'm not ready to explain it.

Lightning continues to flicker in the window, but now that she's distracted, she doesn't even notice the storm. I still hold her close, because I can.

"I miss my dog. His name's Duke."

She frowns, and I know what's coming.

"Duke? As in *university*?"

"As in *Hazard*."

She dissolves into a giggling fit.

"Stop that. I named him when I was nine. By the time I was old enough to realize I had named my beagle after one of Kentucky's biggest basketball rivals, it was too late." I shake my head and sigh. "Anyway, you asked. That's what I miss about home."

"It sounds nice. I've never seen the Appalachian Mountains."

"Never?"

She shakes her head. "Mom worked two jobs. That didn't leave a lot of time for vacations."

"I'd like to show you the mountains."

"I'd like to see them."

"I'm going home for spring break. You should come with me."

The offer slips out before I even realize what I've done. Am I nuts? Taking Steph home to Applewood is the worst possible idea in the world.

Then why does the thought make you so happy?

My mouth goes dry. It's just not possible. Not yet. I'd have to ask my family to keep their mouth shut about the Army.

"I don't know," she says hesitantly. "I wouldn't want to impose on family time. Plus, I planned on spending that week with my mom."

I ignore the disappointment I feel and thank my lucky stars instead.

"I understand."

We sit quietly, wrapped in the blanket and listening to the rain above our heads. Her hand rests on my stomach. She slowly slides her fingers down a little, causing my ab muscles to clench.

"Brandon?"

"Yeah?"

"That no-touching rule is stupid."

"I couldn't agree more."

"Then why haven't you tried to break it?"

"Because it's important to you."

"It's not so important to me anymore."

The blanket drops to the floor as she shifts on my lap.

Facing me. Straddling me.

This is definitely against the rules.

Steph presses her entire body against mine, and my hands automatically find her waist. She shifts again, making us both groan.

Face-to-face.

Heartbeat to heartbeat.

It's torture.

It's heaven.

I close my eyes as she leans in, softly kissing each corner of my mouth. My right hand remains on her hip as the other slides into her hair. She shifts against me again, and I hold her tighter as her lips trail along my neck.

Let her lead.

My body is at war with my mind. I am a twenty-two year old man who has, up until now, desperately tried to be respectful of the boundaries she established. Rules were formed. Lines were drawn in the sand. And I have done everything I can to ignore how much I want her. How much I want to do . . . exactly what we're doing.

Just with less clothes. And maybe on a bed.

"Brandon Walker, stop thinking about it and just kiss me."

"What about the rules?"

"Screw the rules. They were stupid anyway and I nev—"

I kiss her. Hard. She groans and wraps her arms around my neck, pulling me to her until we're as close as we've ever been. For a few fantastic minutes, we're all tongues and hands and moans, because it's been a long time since we've touched and we're both a little worked-up. But after a while, our frantic kisses slow to something much more familiar—something warm and soft and *real*.

We're both breathless when we pull away. And, now, we can actually see each other's faces because at some point, in the middle of the most awesome kiss of my life, the electricity came back on.

And Bangle joined us on the couch.

I eye the cat warily. "She's going to claw my eyes out for touching you."

Steph gives me the sexiest grin I've ever seen before lifting her blouse over her head, letting it fall to the floor.

"Then we better make it worth it," she says.

chapter

fourteen

Stephanie

I don't care that a tornado could be over our heads or that my cat is watching us. I don't even care that I'm wearing my boring, white, cotton bra. All that matters is that Brandon's hands are on my skin and that his eyes are devouring me.

I slide up against him, causing him to grip my hips and hold me still. My mouth latches on to his ear, and the groan that vibrates from his chest causes me to jerk against him. He buries his face against my neck.

"I want this, Brandon. I want you."

"I want you, too."

He swallows my moan with another frantic kiss.

Should I tell him he'll be the first? Is that important to a guy? Or will it turn him off completely? Does he have protection? I certainly don't. Why hadn't I thought about that before *I climbed into his lap and ripped off my shirt?*

He peppers my face with gentle kisses and whispers my name before finding my lips again. This time, the kiss is tender and sweet. It's classic Brandon, and the very reason I love him.

I love him.

Should I tell him?

I hear Mom's voice in my head, telling me to trust my heart.

"I love you, Brandon."

His brown eyes snap open, and I can see the emotion there. His hands frame my face while his thumbs stroke my cheeks.

"I love you, too, Steph."

We smile at each other, and then suddenly, our hands are everywhere, as if our confession gives us permission to do the things we've always wanted to do.

Desperate to feel his skin against mine, I reach for the hem of his cotton tee. We stop kissing just long enough to pull the shirt over his head. I toss it aside and crash my mouth against his. Brandon groans, and I feel his abs tighten beneath my touch as I slide my fingers from his navel up to his chest.

And that's when I feel it.

Cold.

Metallic.

Familiar.

Breaking the kiss, I lean back, and my eyes lock on the ball chain around his neck.

"Steph? What's . . ."

With trembling hands, I reach for the tags. Brandon follows my hands with his eyes, and then he immediately closes them in anguish.

They're his dad's tags. Right?

I take a deep breath and read the engraved print.

Walker. Brandon.

"Steph, I can explain."

Not his dad's.

I stare into his eyes and try to make sense of it, but nothing fits. How could I not know this? Why didn't I feel the tags through his shirt? Why haven't I seen him in his uniform? Is that why he works out every morning? Because he's . . . he's a . . .

My body sways as the room begins to spin. Brandon tightens his arms around me.

"Steph, I swear I wanted to tell you. You have no idea how much I've agonized over it. I just never found the right time, or the right words, because I knew you'd hate me, and I couldn't stand the thought of that because I love you so much. I love you, Steph. I love you so much that I don't even know if I *want* to be a soldier anymore, and I never thought that would happen. It was always the plan. Always. Not forever. I don't want to be a soldier forever, but for now, this is what I am. For the next four years, this is *who* I am."

Tears form in my eyes.

"Say it again."

"I love you."

I shake my head. "Not that, you jerk. Say it."

"Steph, please listen to me."

"Say it!"

He closes his eyes.

"I'm a soldier," he whispers, his voice breaking. "I am a soldier in the United States Army."

In a daze, I climb off his lap and grab my shirt. I pull it on and then walk around the room, blowing out the candles. A thousand questions swirl around in my head, but I don't want to ask them. Because then I'd have to hear his voice, and I don't want to hear his voice anymore.

"Steph, please . . ."

I head to my bedroom, and Brandon follows me down the hallway. I turn around just outside my door.

"Steph . . ."

He reaches for me, but the look on my face must convince him otherwise, because he quickly reconsiders, letting his arms drop to his sides.

"Pack your shit, and get out of my apartment."

And I slam the door in his face.

chapter

fifteen

Stephanie

Three days pass. I only know this because I'm too afraid to let my cell phone die completely. If Mom tried to call me, and I didn't answer, she'd be here in a second, and the last thing I need is my mother.

I don't need anybody.

Not that they haven't tried. My phone's blowing up constantly. Brandon. Tessa. Brandon. Tessa. Xavier. My text messages are insane, and my voicemail is finally, blissfully, full. I did reply to one of Tessa's texts, and I spoke to my mother once, just to let them know I'm alive.

That's all they get.

Bangle has been my constant companion. Animals can sense when their owners are sad. The crumpled wads of tissue probably tipped her off, too.

But I'm all cried out now.

I think.

I hope.

I learned all about the stages of grief in my freshman year psychology class. At the time, I remember thinking that, when it came to my dad, I had avoided feeling the overwhelming sorrow the professor described. And while this doesn't compare to my mom losing my dad, I wonder if she felt this . . . empty. Cold. Betrayed.

I'm hurt and heartbroken. He had so many opportunities to tell me, and he didn't. He moved into my apartment, and let me fall in love with him, knowing how I felt about the military. I feel manipulated. Played for a fool. But no matter how mad I am at Brandon, it doesn't begin to compare to how mad I am at myself.

I knew better. I knew he was too perfect . . . too good to be true.

"I'm a soldier in the United States Army."

The sentence plays on a constant loop inside my head. He could have told me he was a married man and it wouldn't have hit me this hard. I've skipped class, called in sick to work, and haven't touched a bite of food in two days. I'm living on energy drinks and the banana I found at the bottom of my backpack.

I'm disgusted with myself, because I've done the one thing I swore I'd never do.

I let a man break my heart.

My phone chimes. I don't even bother looking at the screen because I simply don't care. It chimes again, and again, until finally I give in and just turn it off. Minutes later, someone pounds on my door. It's not the first time someone has knocked, but it is the first time I hear the door hit the hardwood floor.

Bangle and I both jump off my bed and run into the living room. Xavier's standing there, along with two of the biggest guys I've ever seen.

Wrestlers? Lumberjacks?

"What the hell, Xavier?"

He shrugs. "You wouldn't answer your phone *or* your door. I had my orders."

"Your *orders*? Is your girlfriend seriously so deranged she'd send you over here to break down my door?"

"You better believe she is," Tessa says, stepping inside the apartment. "And we didn't break it down. We just took it off the hinges."

The guys pick up the door and hold it against the jam while Xavier gets to work, replacing the screws.

"You're ridiculous," I mutter, stomping back toward my room.

"*I'm* ridiculous? Your melodramatic ass won't talk to anyone, but I'm the ridiculous one?"

She starts muttering in Spanish, which just pisses me off more because she knows I can't understand a word of it.

Climbing back onto my bed, I clutch a pillow close to my chest.

I will not cry. I will not cry.

"If you must run your mouth, could you at least do it in English? You are supposed to be on my side!"

Tessa sits down on the bed. "I *am* on your side, but I can't support this. *This* is not healthy."

"You don't even know what's going on."

"Sure I do. You found out Brandon's in the Army."

The words cut me like a knife.

"You *knew*?"

"I knew. Xavier knew. Even your mom knew. Are you going to hate *us*, too?"

I'm speechless. Being deceived by Brandon is one thing. Betrayed by my best friends and my mom is a completely different story.

"How did you know?"

"He told me a few weeks ago. Apparently you made him aware of your crazy irrational hatred, and he wanted to know if he would have any chance with you if he came clean. I told him it'd be tricky, but I had no idea you'd be like this. I am so glad you are handling this situation with the maturity of a woman who plans to be a classroom teacher in just a few months. I mean, *damn*."

The tears are rolling now. I reach for the nearest nasty tissue. "What the hell is your point?"

"My point is that this man loves you. *He loves you*! And you love him, and you are turning your back on him because of a commitment he made before he even knew you existed! How is that fair, Steph? How was Brandon supposed to know he would someday meet a girl with this gigantic chip on her shoulder who is so afraid that she'll turn out like her mother that she refuses to open her heart to anyone?"

"You don't know what you're talking about. My mother has nothing to do with this."

Tessa rolls her eyes. "Your mother has *everything* to do with this! You look at your mom and see a miserable woman, but that's not what she is at all. She's broken-hearted, yes. She's lonesome at times, sure. But she is *not* miserable. Through you, she's found a way to move on and live her life. Why can't you do that?"

I shake my head. "I can't love him, Tessa. I won't."

"Too late. You already do."

"I can't. Not anymore."

She sits down next to me and takes my hand. "It's four years of his life, Steph. *Four*. It's not a lifetime. His plan has always been to serve his four years and then find an engineering job, settle down, and have a bunch of kids. And if you want him to make that happen with somebody else, then keep right on doing what you're doing. Keep pushing him away. Because a man will only take so much rejection before he moves on. Do you know how rare it is to find a nice guy who is absolutely crazy about you? Do you have any idea how he feels right now? He can't eat. Can't sleep. Can't work out, and you know how obsessive he was about his morning run. He's a mess."

I had refused to think about how Brandon might be feeling. Or where he was sleeping. Now I know.

"He's staying with you."

Tessa sighs heavily. "Well, of course he's staying with us. You told him to get out. Where else was he supposed to go?"

"Whatever."

"Steph—"

"We were going to have sex. Did he tell you that?"

Her eyes grow wide.

"That's right. We were *this close* to having sex right there on the couch."

Tessa shakes her head. "No, he didn't tell me, which proves the kind of gentleman he really is. What stopped you?"

"Oh, I don't know. Finding his dog tags around his neck sort of killed the mood."

"Wow."

"Yeah. So excuse me if I'm having a hard time feeling sympathetic."

The room grows quiet. Feeling brave, Bangle leaps onto the bed and snuggles close to my side.

"Steph, I'm sorry you found out that way. I really am. But you have to know he had been trying to figure out a way to tell you. He was just so afraid."

"Afraid of what?"

"Afraid of your reaction. Afraid of *this*."

I pull my knees close to my chest. I'm not ready for this. I'm not ready to give him the benefit of the doubt. I'm not ready to understand why he chose to keep me in the dark for so long.

I'm just not ready.

"Steph, you're allowed to feel betrayed. I totally get that. But don't just think about how much you hurt. Think about the way he makes you *feel*. Think about the things he says to you and the way you feel when he touches you. And kisses you. Think about *The Princess Bride* and that New Year's Eve kiss. Think about never feeling the rest of your whole life the way you feel when you're with him."

I smirk. "You totally stole that from *Dirty Dancing*."

"Your fault. You shouldn't have made me watch it a thousand times."

I laugh my first honest laugh in days. She smiles and gives my hand another gentle squeeze.

"I'm so tired, Tessa."

"And hungry, I bet."

"Starving."

"And you need a shower." She smooths the hair away from my face. "Tell you what, you clean up, and I will make you something to eat. Just something light. I'm not sure your stomach can handle anything else. And then I want you to call your mom. We've talked a few times. She's worried about you."

I sniffle and reach for another tissue. "I can't believe she knew, too. She only met him once! How did she figure it out?"

"Something about the way he saluted your dad's tombstone gave him away. I didn't really understand it. You'll have to ask her when you call."

"Okay."

"And then—"

"Don't push it, Tessa."

"And then I want you to *consider* talking to Brandon. Just consider it. He has his reasons for joining the service. And it's not like he has a choice. He is obligated for the next four years. No getting out of it. So if you want him in your life, you will have to find a way to come to terms with that."

"What if I tell you I don't want him in my life?"

"You wouldn't say that."

"How do you know?"

"Because you'd be lying, and you've never lied to me."

I bow my head. She knows me too well.

"Okay. I don't *want* to want him in my life. Better?"

"I don't believe that, either. You've always been so focused. So determined. You had a road map for your life, and so far, you've managed to stay right on track. And then Brandon comes along, and he's unexpected and wonderful and not at all in your plans. Love's like that, you know. It catches you off-guard and throws you for an absolute loop. It's a rollercoaster, full of ups and downs and twists and turns. It can make you sick to your stomach and cause your heart to soar at the very same time. Love is scary and exciting, and it makes you take leaps of faith you swore you'd never take, but you do it. You do it because not having him in your life would be like . . . not having oxygen."

"Now who's being melodramatic? It's not like I need him in order to breathe, Tessa."

She smiles softly and looks around my bedroom.

"Don't you?"

With a heavy sigh, I think about the last few days. I've avoided people, food, work, and school. I have cried and wallowed in my self-pity, and, thanks to my total avoidance of everything and everyone, I've forced my best friend to take the door off the hinges just to make sure I'm alive.

I might be breathing, but I'm not living.

"I think after you shower, eat, and get a good night's sleep, you'll wake up tomorrow with a whole new perspective. Maybe then you'll be ready to listen to what Brandon has to say."

I'm not so sure, but I promise to think about it. She hugs me tight before giving me a stern look and pointing toward the bathroom. With a defeated sigh, I find a set of fresh clothes and head to the shower.

For dinner, Tessa makes chicken noodle soup. It's warm, delicious, and the perfect comfort food. The soup, along with the hot shower, actually makes me feel like a human being again, and we spend the rest of the day snuggled under a blanket on the couch, watching a marathon of *The Golden Girls.*

Don't judge. We both love Betty White.

It's late in the evening when Tessa finally hands me my cell phone.

"I'd hoped you'd forgotten," I mutter.

"Not a chance. Call your mother."

"I don't know what to say to her."

"You probably won't have to say much."

Great. "I'm not in the mood for a lecture, either."

"I know, but I really think you need to listen to what she has to say."

Tessa gives me a hug, and I slowly make my way to my bedroom. Closing the door behind me, I collapse on the bed and pull the blanket over me before tapping the screen.

Mom answers on the first ring. "So you are alive."

"I am."

We both sigh at the same time. It's almost comical.

Almost.

"Stephanie—"

"Why didn't you tell me?"

A few seconds pass before she answers.

"It wasn't my place to tell you. Brandon had his reasons for keeping you in the dark. He was afraid of your reaction, and boy, did you prove him right."

"Well, maybe if someone had told me the truth from the very begin—"

"Stephanie, it wouldn't have mattered when you found out the truth. Your reaction would have been exactly like this. I knew that. Brandon knew it, too. Any sane person would have wanted to avoid this for as long as possible."

"So you're on his side."

Mom sighs softly. "You are so much like your father."

"I'll take that as a compliment."

"Don't. His stubbornness was his least attractive quality."

My mouth snaps shut. It's the first time my mom has ever said anything remotely negative about my dad.

"Stephanie, you are an adult now. It's time you learn that sometimes, there are no *sides*. Everything isn't always black and white. Sometimes, there's gray."

"But I don't like gray. I like knowing what's right and wrong. I like knowing what's real and what's phony. And Brandon is—"

"Brandon is your gray," Mom says softly. "The grays are the parts of your life that mold you into the woman you are meant to be. The little, unexpected surprises that catch you completely off guard. Your experiences, your reactions, your feelings . . . they're all important because they shape you. For too long, you've lived on a very safe and secure course. You had a plan, and you've followed it to the letter. Now that something has come along to completely knock you off track, you're handling it very immaturely. And that's my fault."

I choose to ignore that my mom just called me immature. I'm too devastated by the fact that she thinks she failed as a mother.

"You're a great mom. The very best."

"Not if this is the way you treat the people you love when they disappoint you. I thought I taught you to be compassionate. I can't believe I raised a daughter who refuses to give someone she claims to love the benefit of the doubt."

"*Claims* to love? You think I don't love him?"

"I don't know. Do you?"

It's a challenge. A gauntlet thrown.

"Stephanie, when you visited, you told me it wasn't serious, but it *could* be. You said nothing about loving him."

"Well, I do. I love him."

"Hmm. So you weren't completely honest with me?"

"I didn't lie . . ."

"That's not what I asked."

Not to brag, but I'm a pretty smart girl. I can totally tell when my mom has just given me a taste of my own medicine. I'm about to protest that it's not the same thing, but I don't waste my breath, because I know in my heart that it is. Granted, I didn't directly ask Brandon if he was in the military, just like Mom didn't come right out and ask if I was in love with him. But in both situations, neither of us told the whole truth.

"Sweetheart, you've always been afraid to get close to anyone. The only positive, loving relationship you've ever really been around is Tessa and Xavier's, for heaven's sake. Maybe if I'd remarried . . ."

I'm stunned at the thought that maybe Mom had met someone she might have wanted to spend her life with. "Did you ever want to remarry?"

Mom laughs softly. "No. I've always believed you have one great love, and I'd had mine. And, if I'm being honest, I was afraid to love again. You know that quote, 'Tis better to have loved and lost than never to have loved at all?' "

159

"Yeah. Alfred Lord Tennyson said that."

"Well, that may be true, but I had already survived one heartbreak. I wasn't about to risk it again."

Sighing heavily, I roll over onto my back and stare at the ceiling.

"What do I do, Mom?"

"I can't tell you what to do. But I can tell you what *not* to do. Don't give up on him. You see, I didn't need you tell me that you're in love with him. He wouldn't have been sitting in our house—on the anniversary of your father's death—if you didn't. I knew you'd tell me when you could find the words. Maybe that's what Brandon was trying to do. Maybe he was just trying to find the words."

"I wonder if he's found them."

"I don't know. But if he has, I think you should listen to him."

We hang up, and before I completely lose my nerve, I find my jacket and head to the living room. A smiling Tessa's already standing at the door, with a plastic container in her hand.

"Take these with you. Trust me. Brandon will love them."

I smirk and sneak a peek under the lid.

"When did you have time to bake?"

"Chocolate sandwich cookies are no-bake and take less than fifteen minutes. I *couldn't* let you go over there empty-handed. It's Valentine's Day!"

Holy crap. "And you're *here*? Why aren't you with Xavier?"

"He's at a game. Besides, I'm with him every night. You needed me."

I hug her tight. "You're the best friend ever."

"I know."

"But *this* . . ." I shake the container of cookies, ". . . doesn't mean anything. I'm just going over there to listen to what he has to say."

"Got it."

"I'm serious."

"I know."

Tessa gives me a wink, and I take a deep breath before taking my cookies and heading out into the chilly February night.

chapter

sixteen

Brandon

I had no idea television could be so stupid, especially on a holiday. Every freaking channel is showing some puke-worthy romantic movie that reminds losers like me that it's Valentine's Day. Without a basketball game on anywhere, my choices are limited to hockey (which I hate) and European soccer (which I hate even more).

You should have gone to the game with Xavier.

Probably, but that would have required a shower and leaving this room—neither of which I'm interested in doing.

I settle on watching *Top Gun* and toss the remote aside. Unfortunately, it's the scene in the bar when the guys are singing 'You've Lost that Lovin' Feeling,' which does nothing to improve my shitty mood.

I bet this is the one 80s movie I won't find in Steph's collection.

With a groan, I grab the remote and turn it off. The room is instantly filled with darkness, which is exactly how I like it. Tessa doesn't, though, so out of respect for her and the fact that she's allowed me to be an absolute bum for the past three days, I turn on the bedside lamp. The light is too bright, but she says sitting in the dark is sad and depressing.

Lord knows I wouldn't want to be depressed.

After countless ignored texts and unanswered voice mails, I'm in that weird period in a break-up where you're just pissed at everything. I don't know that I can even call it a *break-up*. Were we even together? We'd never really discussed it. Steph and I had just fallen into this easy, comfortable dance. Stupidly, I thought the dance would end with me telling her the truth, and by then, she'd be so in love with me she wouldn't care that I was a soldier.

It was a stupid plan. Idiotic, even.

For the first time in my life, I had allowed my heart to rule my head. Just like my sister feared, I'd lost my focus and let a girl become more important than everything else.

The best thing you can do for yourself and Steph is forget that she exists. You'll just break her heart, and doing that will break yours."

My sister's words haunt me. Somehow, Christian knew how this would turn out. She realized what a mess I'd make.

Speaking of missed calls . . .

I scroll through my phone. Christian's called several times today, but I've let them all go to voice mail. I can't talk to her. Not yet. She'd hear my voice, and she'd know. And I'm just not in the mood to hear how she told me so.

I've got to get a grip. I know this. I'm skipping class and my early morning runs, and I'm dodging phone calls from Ms. Linda, which means I've probably lost my job at the coffee shop. I only go to PT because they'll kick me out of the program if I don't. Telling my family—and especially my father—that I've been dismissed from the ROTC program would be the ultimate disappointment, and I won't do that to them.

They shouldn't suffer just because I'm an idiot.

My stomach growls, reminding me it hasn't seen food in three days. Knowing I have the apartment to myself and won't have to deal with their pitiful looks, I finally emerge from the guest bedroom and head to the kitchen.

Xavier and Tessa are good friends. I'm thankful, because without them, I'd be back at my old apartment. The guys would ask too many questions. At least Xavier and Tessa already know the answers, so they didn't give me any crap. Xavier simply offered me the guest room for as long as I wanted it and told me to make myself at home. And God bless Tessa. She's tried everything in the world to convince me to eat. Last night, she'd even found a recipe for Kentucky barbeque chicken, hoping something that reminded me of home would actually give me an appetite.

It didn't.

I'd spilled my guts, and while neither of them had seemed too surprised at Steph's reaction, I could tell they felt sorry for me. Fewer things piss me off than someone's pity, but in this case, it was warranted because I was, and still am, a mess.

I broke her heart, and in the process, I broke mine, too.

Just like my sister said I would.

After making myself a sandwich, I hunt in the fridge for a bottle of water before sitting down at the island. I've barely taken my first bite when I hear a knock at the door. I ignore it and force myself to take another bite. The knocking continues, and continues, until finally, I toss my sandwich in the trash and head to the living room.

I don't even bother looking through the peephole.

"Who the—"

My mouth goes dry. Steph's standing there with red cheeks and wind-blown hair. Breathless and beautiful.

"Hey," she whispers.

"Hi."

We just stand there, staring at each other. She looks exhausted, and I wonder if she's slept at all.

"You look tired."

"So do you."

I nod. I can't imagine how scruffy I look. But I can't think about that right now. All I can think about is that she's here. Then I remember she hates me, and she's just here to see her friend.

"Tessa's not here. Xavier's gone, too."

Steph nods. "I know. She spent the day with me. She . . . forced me to take a shower and eat some soup. Oh, and call my mom. That was a fun conversation."

I have no idea what to say. *Why is she here?*

"Can I come in?" Her voice is soft and fragile, and that's when I realize she's nervous. Stunned, I step aside, and Steph walks into the living room. We follow each other over to the couch.

"I brought cookies," she says as she sits down. "Tessa insisted. Something about it being Valentine's Day and I couldn't come over here empty-handed."

I grin and sit down next to her. "Food is Tessa's answer to everything."

"Yeah." She hands me the cookies, and I open the container. "I have no idea what they are. Chocolate Sandwich . . . *somethings*. I wasn't really paying attention. I'm sure they're delicious, though."

I place the lid back on the plastic container and set it aside. "I'm sure they are."

"Yeah." Steph looks down at her hands. "Tessa said you haven't been eating. Or sleeping. Or working out."

"I've worked out some. PT requires it."

"PT?"

"Physical Training. It's just three days a week. It's this list of events that I need to complete in order to pass the Army's Physical Fitness Test. There's a minimum score on each event, so that's why I run every day."

"Oh. What are the events?"

She actually sounds interested. Maybe she just doesn't know what else to say. Or maybe she's stalling. I'd spent so much time avoiding the subject with her I find that I'm actually excited to talk about it.

"Push-ups, sit-ups, and the two mile run."

"I bet you're fast, with all the running you do."

"It's actually my best event."

She nods. The desire to touch her is making me a little crazy, but I'm not a complete idiot. Instead, I reach for the container and rip off the lid.

"Steph, do you want a cook—?"

"Why is this so awkward?"

Sighing heavily, I replace the lid and set the cookies on the end table.

"I mean, we've never been *awkward*," she says softly. "We were easy. Comfortable. We never ran out of things to say or talk about. Everything with you was just . . ."

"Effortless."

"Yeah."

"It's awkward now because I made it awkward. I kept something very important from you. Something I should have told you from the very beginning, and I didn't. I still don't know how. Before you, the Army was all that mattered to me, and I talked about it constantly. The fact that I never mentioned it to you still blows my mind. But then you told me you could never date a soldier, and I knew right then that I had to keep my mouth shut. For a little while, anyway. That's why I volunteered to be your roommate. Yes, I needed a place to stay, but I really just wanted to spend more time with you so I could prove that I was . . . a good guy, I guess."

"Brandon, you didn't have to prove that to me. I knew you were a good guy the night I sprained my ankle and you basically carried me home."

"But it wasn't enough. If I had told you I was a soldier, the exact same thing would have happened then that's happening now. You would have hated me."

She shakes her head. "I don't hate you, Brandon. This would be so much easier if I did."

I don't know what to say to that, so I just wait for her to continue.

"You were not in my plans," Steph says softly. "As my mom and Tessa pointed out so many times today, I had a very distinct idea of what this year would involve. School. Work. Graduation. My only goal was to get my degree and find a teaching job. Falling in love with you was not on my list of things to do."

"And falling in love with a soldier is pretty much your worst nightmare."

"Pretty much."

She bows her head and sniffles softly. Unable to keep my hands to myself a minute longer, I slide closer and kiss her shoulder. Her cheek. Her temple. Like always, she smells like peaches and cream, and she melts against me.

"I'm sorry, Steph. I'm sorry."

Her tears fall quietly, and I feel like the biggest asshole in the world, because I made her cry. She's crying because I love her, and because she loves me, and the last thing she wants to do is love me.

"Tell me what to do," I whisper against her hair.

She takes a deep, steadying breath and turns her head toward me.

"Tell me why you want to be a soldier."

Such a simple request. Too bad the answer is so freaking complicated. It's impossible to explain why I want to be a soldier without telling her about my dad's condition. *Will this be just one more secret I've kept from her? Another lie to add to my mile-long list?*

"You know my dad served in Vietnam."

She nods.

"The military was his life. Even after he retired, he made no secret that he expected me to follow in his footsteps. My sister was daddy's little girl, and she had him wrapped around her finger. It wasn't as easy for me to please my father. I knew becoming a soldier would make him proud, so joining the service was always the plan. I didn't care, because I had no idea what I wanted to do with my life. But as I got older, I started messing with computers. I loved taking them apart and putting them back together. By the time I was fifteen, I had built my first PC with just scraps and parts. It was during my senior year of high school that I told Dad I wanted to major in computer engineering. He was fine with it, because he knew, just like I did, that I could join ROTC. I would graduate with my engineering degree *and* as an officer in the Army. Plus, my tuition would be covered. It was the perfect solution. Or, I thought it was."

Steph reaches for my hand. "What's changed?"

"I want to make my family proud, and I still want to be a soldier, but doing it forever no longer appeals to me. It never did, to be honest. As you've probably noticed, I have a problem with making snap decisions without really considering the long-term consequences."

Steph laces her fingers with mine. "So joining ROTC is iron-clad? There's no getting out of it?"

"Not for me. I received an ROTC scholarship, and that requires a four-year commitment. I wouldn't want to get out of it, anyway. I will finish what I started. I owe that much to my father. Especially now." I swallow down the emotion that threatens to bubble up from my throat. "About three years ago, Dad was diagnosed with early Alzheimer's. He started misplacing his keys. He lost interest in fishing—something he always loved to do. Just little things that we blamed on stubbornness and old age. We had no idea . . ."

"Oh, Brandon. I didn't know."

Of course she didn't. How could she?

"When I was home for Christmas, all he talked about was how proud he was of me. That he couldn't wait to watch me graduate as a second lieutenant in May. My father can't remember the day of the week, but he remembers that his only son is joining the military." I take a deep breath and look into her tear-filled eyes. "So you see, even if I could get out of my commitment, I wouldn't. Not even for you. And that's hard for me to admit, because there's pretty much nothing I wouldn't do for you."

Steph places her palm against my cheek. "You made a promise to your father. You should honor it."

With those words, relief courses through me.

She understands. She really understands.

"You are an amazing man, and I am so in love with you."

"I love you, too. You said I wasn't in your plans. I wasn't expecting you, either. Joining the Army was easy because there was nothing holding me here. Nothing to make me second-guess my decision. I've done nothing but agonize over it since you told me how you felt. My sister said the best thing I could do for both our sakes was forget you exist, but by that time, I was already crazy about you. I knew I'd have to tell you eventually. I was just trying to figure out a way that didn't end with you hating my guts for the rest of my life."

Steph takes a deep breath and snuggles close to my side.

"Brandon, what happens after graduation?"

"I'll have a few weeks leave before reporting to Fort Gordon, Georgia for AIT. Signal Corps Training. It's twelve weeks."

"And after that?"

"I don't know. I could be sent to another base to manage their network systems. Or, I could be sent out with my unit on specific missions. The possibilities are endless. I won't know until close to graduation from AIT."

She nods and bows her head.

With a sigh, I kiss her temple. "Please don't hate me."

"I don't hate you. I'm just very, very afraid."

"What are you afraid of?"

I watch her face as she carefully chooses her words. "I have to be honest. I . . . don't know that I can do this. I know I should try. I should be a grown-up, follow my heart, and ignore my fears. But anytime I think about doing that, all I see is my mother. The widow. The woman who lost her husband before she was legally old enough to drink away her sorrows. I love you, and I'm going to keep falling in love with you."

"I love you, too, Steph—"

"But you're leaving. Soldiers leave, and sometimes, they don't come back."

Her voice breaks, and I hold her tighter against me. I don't say anything. What can I say? *I'll always come home?* Those words would be a complete insult to the memory of her father. I can't make her any promises. Not one. And it makes me sick to my stomach.

"You don't know where you'll be. We've made no real commitment to each other, and maybe we never will. Maybe you don't even want to—"

"I want to."

She sighs and wipes her cheek. "I don't know if I can, and I don't want to make you a promise I can't keep. I just . . . I need some time. I need to think."

It's not a *no*. It's not a *never*. It's a chance. A possibility.

"I can do that, Steph. I can give you time."

"Thank you." She smiles at me before looking out the window at the darkening sky. "I should probably go."

I place another kiss along her temple before she slips out of my arms. We stand, and I follow her to the door. As she zips her jacket, I consider kissing her. But I realize that sweet temple kisses are probably okay. Really kissing her is probably not an option right now.

"Thank you for the cookies."

"You're welcome. Happy Valentine's Day, Brandon."

"Happy Valentine's Day."

Steph steps out into the hallway. I'm just about to close the door when she turns back around.

"Aren't you coming?" she asks.

My pulse quickens. *Is she serious?*

Steph fidgets with her jacket sleeve. "I mean, I know I told you to get out, but you still need a place to stay, and I still need a roommate. I'm sure Tessa and Xavier told you to stay as long as you like, but I really think you should come home. That is, if you want to."

The need to kiss her nearly suffocates me now, but I know it's out of the question. And that's okay. Because I have a chance, and it's more than I could have ever hoped for.

I smile. "I would love to come home."

chapter seventeen

Stephanie

For the next few days, Brandon is true to his word and gives me space. There are no stolen kisses or tender touches. No sweet text messages or sappy voice mails. Most mornings, he's out the door before I wake up and in bed by the time I get home from class or the library.

But we'll see each other today, because today is Women's Lit.

Thanks to the stupid torrential downpour that began just as I was leaving the apartment, I'm running late. By the time I reach the lecture hall, there's only one seat left, and of course, it's in the back row, right next to Brandon.

This should be sufficiently awkward.

I sit down in the seat next to him, but his eyes are glued to his phone. Even when the teacher begins her lecture, he doesn't look up. She starts handing out last week's tests, and I nudge his shoulder. Brandon looks up and blinks rapidly before his eyes finally focus on me.

"What's wrong?" I whisper.

He sighs heavily. "I was just reading an e-mail from my sister."

"Oh. Is something wrong?"

"Dad's not doing so well. Christian wants me to come home for spring break."

"You planned to, didn't you?"

"Yeah, but she never *asks* me to come home. She's always trying to get me to go to the beach or something. You know, normal spring break stuff. But I always go home. The fact that she's asking is probably not a good sign. I need to call her."

As class continues, I notice Brandon's knee jumping. Desperate to calm him down, I reach over and place my hand on his leg. It's probably inappropriate, considering our current situation, but I can't stand to see him so nervous.

After a few minutes, his leg stills. I hear him take a deep breath before placing his hand over mine, which is where it remains until the teacher dismisses us.

I'm sitting on the couch when Brandon finally emerges from his bedroom. He's spent the last two hours in there, and I don't know if the call lasted that long or if he'd just needed some privacy afterward.

"I saved you some dinner."

"Thanks." His voice is weary as he collapses on the couch. "I don't think I can eat, though."

"Do you want to talk about it?"

He rubs his face tiredly. "Dad's dementia has progressed to the point that the doctor thinks it won't be long until his daily care will require more than Christian can handle on her own. My sister, the nurse, who is the strongest woman I've ever known, broke down while telling me that on Dad's worse days—and there have been many lately—he doesn't even know her name. She says she needs me to come home to help her hire a full-time nurse, but that can't be the reason. She's the RN. I don't know the first thing about any of this."

"I don't think she needs your help. She probably just needs her brother."

He nods. "She's having to be a nurse 24/7, and it's killing her. Plus, she has two little girls. I should be there. I should be helping take care of our family."

I wrap my arms around him and hug him tight. With a shuddering breath, he buries his face against my neck. His shoulders shake, and I gently stroke his back. I know he's crying, and it breaks my heart.

When he lifts his head, I pretend not to notice the tears on his cheeks.

"I'd like to help. Let me come with you."

His brow furrows. "Steph, you don't have to do that."

"I know. I want to. Besides, you promised to show me the mountains."

Brandon smiles and brushes a strand of hair away from my face.

"I did promise that," he says.

I take his hands in mine. "You met my dad. I'd like to meet yours."

"Even if he's hateful and mean and—"

"Even if."

He leans forward and touches my forehead with his.

"Okay," he murmurs.

"Okay."

The five-hour drive to Applewood, Kentucky is mostly by interstate, making it a fairly boring drive for Brandon. I, however, am amazed. Especially when the freeways turn into two-lane roads with big rolling hills and dark wooden fences that line mile after mile of the countryside.

Brandon laughs at my excitement. "Don't tell me you've never seen a horse before."

"Shut up. They're beautiful."

Brandon chuckles. "They are. I've just lived in the country so long I guess I'm immune to it."

I gaze out the window. "How far is it to your house?"

"About ten more miles."

Brandon taps his fingers on the steering wheel, but there's no music.

"Why are you nervous?"

He turns his head in my direction. "What makes you think I'm nervous?"

I roll my eyes.

"Fine, I'm nervous. I don't really know what to expect at home. I just hope Dad's having a good day, and I hope my sister . . ."

His voice trails off as he makes a right turn onto a gravel road.

"You hope your sister . . ."

Brandon sighs. "I just hope she's on her best behavior."

"What does that mean?"

"It means that she had some very strong opinions about you and me, and she probably won't roll out the welcome mat."

"Seriously? And you planned on telling me this when?"

"I'm telling you now."

Unbelievable. This trip has been planned for three weeks, and we've just spent more than five hours in this truck, and *now* he's telling me this?

"What's her problem with me?"

"Her problem isn't with *you*, necessarily. She was just worried about the same thing you were worried about—that living together would be a distraction to graduating on time. And she was worried that I would break your heart. Which I did."

I can't look at him. If I did, he'd see the tears that had suddenly formed in my eyes, and I don't want him to see that. I just stare out at the pretty scenery instead.

"She knows everything?"

"Yes."

Great. "I bet she hates me."

"Why would she hate you?"

I quickly wipe my cheek. "Because I broke your heart, too."

We don't say anything else, but he reaches for my hand, and our fingers remain laced until we come upon an off-white, two-story house out in the middle of nowhere. It's surrounded by what was probably at one time a matching white picket fence. Both are in need of a fresh coat of paint. Despite its outward appearance, it's beautiful, with a wrap-around porch and wooden swing swaying in the breeze. The house is surrounded by snow-covered mountains and dirt roads, and I find myself instantly falling in love with it.

I don't notice that Brandon has turned off the ignition until he squeezes my hand.

"Not what you expected? I know it looks a little rough on the outside, but—"

"Actually, it's everything I expected. And everything I didn't."

His brow furrows. "What does that mean?"

"You've seen where I grew up. I had friends with big, beautiful houses, just like this one, with a gigantic porch and swing. This is sort of my dream house, to be honest. I didn't expect that."

Brandon grins. "Good. Ready to see the inside?"

Am I? I can't deny I'm nervous. I'm meeting his family, after all. And from what I've been told, his sister may not be thrilled to see me. But more importantly, inside those walls is a family that's dealing with many forms of sadness and loss. A father struggles just to remember the day of the week, and a daughter tries to take care of him while raising two little girls on her own.

And your biggest problem is that you're in love with a soldier. Kind of puts things in perspective, doesn't it?

But this trip is not about me. I'm here for Brandon, just like he was there for me at the graveyard, and it's that knowledge that gives me the courage to climb out of the truck.

Brandon takes my hand, and we grab our bags before walking together up the steps and onto the porch. He doesn't bother knocking. Just walks right in, and we're immediately greeted by the excited barking of the sweetest looking dog I've ever seen.

"Hey, boy," Brandon says, dropping his bag. He kneels to the ground to let the dog jump all over him. I've always been a cat person, so the loud barking and constant leaping is a shock to my system and does little to calm my nerves. But the happiness on Brandon's face is worth it.

Suddenly, a woman's voice makes me jump.

"Duke! Why are you bark—" Her voice trails off just as she appears from around the corner. She stops abruptly and wipes her hand on the apron tied around her waist. "Oh! You made good time."

"Very little traffic," Brandon says, rising to his feet. "Hey, Sis."

They share an affectionate hug.

"Christian, I want you to meet Steph."

Christian offers her hand. "Nice to meet you, Steph. I've heard a lot about you."

There's a smile on her face, but there's nothing warm about it. I decide to play along and force a smile, too. We shake hands, and it's completely awkward and uncomfortable. Brandon doesn't notice because he's back on the floor with his dog.

"Dinner will be in about an hour," Christian says.

"It's too quiet. Where are the girls?"

"With their father. It's their spring break, too. Unfortunately, the custody agreement says he gets to keep them all week. He did agree to let them come by tomorrow to see you."

"How nice of him," Brandon says. I can tell by his tone he doesn't care for Christian's ex. "What about Dad? Where's he?"

"Napping in the recliner."

"Good day?"

Christian eyes me. "So far."

Yep, she hates me.

"Okay. We'll let him sleep. I'm gonna show Steph around."

"I made up the guest room for her."

"Thank you," I tell her, but she's already headed back to the kitchen.

Brandon turns toward me. "Well, that wasn't so bad. Come on. Let's get unpacked."

Reaching down for my bag, I let out a deep breath and follow him upstairs. My room, the guest room, is the last door on the left.

"Right next to mine," he says with a wink.

I laugh and roll my eyes before stepping inside. It's pretty, with a mint-green bedspread and matching curtains. The walls are fairly bare, except for a few family photos hanging here and there. A small television sits on top of the dresser.

"Do you want some privacy while you unpack?" Brandon asks.

"Nah. I don't really have that much. Just some sweatshirts and jeans."

I unpack quickly, and then we head to his bedroom. The first things I notice are the trophies and plaques lining the wall across from his bed.

"Did you play sports?"

"Basketball. I wasn't very good."

"Hmm. All these trophies would suggest otherwise."

"Nah, I just had good teammates."

I can tell he's embarrassed, so I let it go and sit down on his bed while he finishes unpacking. With a quiet sigh, I trail my hand across his blue comforter. Sitting on his bed conjures images in my mind that shouldn't be there, especially when we're in his father's house. Desperate for a distraction, I stare at the posters on his walls and the books on his shelf.

"That's a lot of books. Who's your favorite author?"

He doesn't answer. I look up to find him standing there, staring at me with a look on his face I can't even begin to describe. But just because I can't describe it doesn't mean I can't feel it. Whatever he's thinking and feeling radiates from him, and it's all I can do not to jump into his arms.

I swallow nervously. "Why are you staring?"

"Because you look good on my bed. Like you belong there." Brandon shakes his head. "I'm sorry. I know that probably sounds awful, but—"

"It doesn't sound awful."

Closing his eyes, he takes a deep breath before turning back to his closet.

This is what you wanted, Steph. Time and space. Remember?

I do us both a favor and climb off the bed.

While he finishes unpacking, I walk over to his bookshelf and scan the titles. Hawthorne. Twain. Falkner. I even spot some more modern stuff by John Grisham and Stephen King. There seems to be no rhyme or reason to the arrangement of the books, which the little librarian in me finds troubling.

A picture frame on the wall catches my eye. It's a young woman, holding a baby in her lap while a dark-haired toddler stands at her side. The woman's eyes are deep brown. I don't even have to ask who she is.

"Your mom was beautiful. What's her name?"

"Diana." Brandon walks over to me and glances up at the photograph. "She was beautiful. This picture's deceiving, though."

"Is it?"

"Yeah, but I think that's why it's my favorite. I mean, look at her. Doesn't she look like she actually loves her kids?"

"Brandon, I'm sure she—"

"We should probably go help my sister with dinner."

The expression on his face is clear. The subject of his mother is off limits. Not that I blame him. I'd hate her, too.

"Okay."

He visibly relaxes. With a smile, he takes my hand and leads me out of his room.

chapter eighteen

Brandon

Once we're downstairs, Steph asks me to point her to the bathroom. I'm not sure if it's really necessary or if she's just trying to give me a few moments alone with my sister, but either way, I'm thankful. There is something I need to say to Christian, and I really don't want Steph to hear it.

"Smells good in here."

Christian looks up from the stove. "Nothing fancy. Just chicken. Would you mind setting the table?"

"Sure." I head toward the cabinet in search of plates and glasses. "Listen, I want to talk to you about Steph. She's important to me, so I'm going to need you to chill out while we're here."

"Hey, I smiled at the girl. I even put fresh sheets on the bed. I think I'm being downright civil."

I roll my eyes and set the table.

"I still don't understand why you brought her home, Brandon. You aren't together, right?"

"I told you. She's here as my friend."

"Whatever. You are completely in love with her."

"So?"

"*So*? Have you forgotten how she feels about you?"

"She loves me. It's the military she hates."

Christian snorts. "Loving you means loving *all* of you, Brandon. Can she do that?"

"I don't know. We're working on it."

"How are you working on it?"

"She asked for time, and I'm giving it to her."

"And your idea of giving her time is to bring her home to meet the family?"

What the hell is this?

"Christian, did you ask me to come home just to give me shit about my girlfriend? Because I don't need this. We can leave now and make it to the beach by dawn."

We glare angrily at each other until a noise from the living room makes us both jump. I take off running, only to stop abruptly when I turn the corner and find Steph on the couch, sitting right next to my now wide-awake father as he lounges in his recliner.

"There's my son!" Dad beams. "This sweet girl was just helping me find the remote."

"You just knocked it off the arm of your chair." Steph hands him the remote before looking up at me, smiling sheepishly. "Sorry, it sounded kind of heated in there, so I took a detour."

"And I'm glad she did. Now get over here and officially introduce me to this pretty girl."

I sit down next to Steph and make the introductions. Dad seems to be in a great mood. And lucid, which isn't what I expected at all. He looks as if he's lost a little weight, but otherwise, he doesn't appear that much different than when I was home for Christmas.

"So you're Brandon's girlfriend?"

Steph glances at me. I shrug uselessly. Explaining our complicated relationship would surely make my dad's head explode.

"Yeah, I'm his girlfriend."

I know she's just being practical. *Girlfriend* is easy to comprehend. Not that it matters. He probably won't even remember this conversation tomorrow.

Before I let that thought depress me too much, I smile at the two of them. "Dinner's almost ready. Want to head into the kitchen?"

Dad's balance isn't the greatest, so I take him by the arm and lead him toward the kitchen. Once we're at the table, Dad insists on sitting next to Steph, which infuriates my sister since that particular seat has been hers since we were kids.

After the food is passed around and everyone digs in, Dad begins to grill Steph about every detail of her life. Where is she from? What's her major? Does she want to be a teacher in elementary school or high school? It's not new information to me, but that doesn't make it any less fascinating. The two most important people in my life are having a conversation, and if the smiles on their faces are any indication, they're actually enjoying it.

After a while, I sneak a glance at Christian. Anyone with eyes can see that my sister's tired. But I'm not just anyone, and being her brother gives me better eyesight than most. Christian is beyond tired. She's exhausted. Fed up. Drained dry. And it kills me because she's just twenty-six years old. Her deadbeat ex-husband is at least helping her with the girls, but it's not enough—not when you have a full-time nursing job and a father who will soon require around-the-clock care. Christian watches Steph and Dad's exchange with a frown on her face. I can't tell if it's jealousy, rage, or simply disbelief. Probably a little of all three. When you combine all that with her complete exhaustion, it's easy to see why she's in such a pissy mood.

"How's school going for you, Brandon? Grades still good?"

The question doesn't surprise me. Dad always wants a play-by-play of my classes and GPA.

"So far, so good."

"I'm glad to hear that. I was a little worried when Christian said you were bringing a girl home." Dad glances at Steph. "Nothing personal, sweetheart. Brandon can just get easily distracted if his sister and I don't keep him in line."

Steph nods and sips her sweet tea.

Christian places her fork on her plate. "Yeah. It's very important that Brandon stays focused. We wouldn't want anything to get in the way of him graduating on time."

"That's right," Dad says with a nod. "We soldier on, no matter what. Right, son?"

"Right, Dad."

Steph stabs at her chicken, which naturally, my sister notices.

"Something wrong with your dinner, Steph?"

I find my sister's foot under the table and give it a kick.

Steph looks up from her plate and smiles politely. Even I can tell it's forced.

"The chicken's great."

"Then why aren't you eating it?"

"Maybe I'm full."

"Oh, you're definitely full of something."

"Stop it, Christian," I mutter under my breath.

She ignores me.

"Tell us, Steph. What do you think about Brandon's career plans? Surely you have an opinion about that."

The girls stare at each other with daggers in their eyes.

"You already know my opinion. Otherwise, you wouldn't be asking." Steph tosses her napkin on the table and quickly stands up. "Thanks for dinner. I'm going for a walk."

I wait until I hear the front door slam before turning toward my sister.

"Listen to me very carefully because I will not repeat myself. I am home because you asked me to come home, but I will not stay if you insist on being a bitch to her all week long."

She rolls her eyes and rises from her chair. "Whatever. I'm going to help our father with his medication and get him to bed. You know, our father? The one whose heart you're going to break if you don't keep your promise?"

"I have every intention of keeping my promise. And stop talking about him like he isn't here."

"He *isn't* here, Brandon! Look at him!"

I take a deep breath and look over at my dad. He's just staring out the window. His expression blank. His eyes empty. And I know we've lost him. He's gone, deep in the black hole of dementia that sneaks up out of nowhere and steals him away from us.

For the first time I'm thankful for it, because I don't want him to remember any of this.

Christian takes Dad by the arm, helping him to his feet.

Dad blinks rapidly. "Is dinner over?"

"Yeah, it's over," Christian says gently.

Dad doesn't even look my way as Christian leads him to his room.

With a heavy sigh, I grab my jacket and zip it up before heading outside. I expect to find Steph sitting in the porch swing, but she's nowhere to be found. Stuffing my hands in my pockets, I walk along the long porch and lean against the railing, looking out across the grass that still has a thin dusting of snow on it.

It might be spring break according to the calendar, but the mountains sometimes take a little longer to thaw out.

There's really only one place she could be, so I step off the porch and walk around to the back of the house. I look off in the distance toward my dad's pond, and she's there, sitting on the wooden deck. Dad always said the pond was his favorite place on earth, and we spent countless hours each spring and summer fishing or swimming in it. As I approach the water, I notice it's still slightly frozen over, but that doesn't stop my dog from jumping right into it. And then jumping right back out.

Dumb dog.

I sit down next to Steph. "It's cold out here."

"It's colder in there."

I can't deny it.

"You should have told me she hates me. I could have prepared myself."

"She doesn't hate you. She's just bitter about everything in general. She's probably a little afraid of you, too."

"Because I'm *so* scary."

"You are. You're the first girl I've ever brought home. She knows that means something, and I think it terrifies her."

Duke chooses that moment to jump in and out of the pond once again.

"My dog is stupid, by the way."

Steph laughs. "Do you think he forgets the water's cold?"

"Nah, he's just dumb."

She chuckles softly and looks out across the water.

"Steph, I'm sorry about my sister. She has a lot of worries that a twenty-six-year-old shouldn't have. She's a single-mom, a full-time nurse at work, a full-time nurse at *home* . . . it's just a lot for her to juggle alone. But none of that is your fault, so please don't think I'm making excuses for her. And I just told her that if she's going to insist on being a bitch the entire time we're here, we won't be staying."

"Brandon, you should stay. You said your leave after graduation will be a short one. You need to spend every minute you can with them."

"I can take you home and come back. It's just a few hours."

Steph tilts her head in my direction. "Am I really the first girl you ever brought home?"

"Yes."

Our bodies are just barely touching, but I can't resist reaching for her. I slip my arm around her, and she snuggles close to my side.

"You said the fact that you brought me home means something. What does it mean?"

"It means I'm seriously in love with you."

Steph smiles at me. She doesn't say it back. She doesn't have to. The fact that she's here proves it.

"Then I can't give her the satisfaction of running me off, can I?"

I chuckle and kiss her temple. "That's my girl."

Her eyes flicker to my mouth, making my stomach clench with want as she leans forward. We haven't kissed in so long. It's crazy that I'm actually nervous.

But then she kisses me, and all my anxiety is gone. Everything about her is sweet and warm. Her body as she leans against me. Her lips as they touch mine. Even the little moan that vibrates from her when I slide my hands into her hair and deepen the kiss.

We're both breathless when we come up for air.

"I am, you know," she whispers. "I'm your girl. I know I've made it awkward and weird, but I've never stopped being yours. Not in my heart, anyway."

"Not in mine, either." I smile and trail my finger along her cold cheek.

"I'm trying, Brandon. I'm trying to make my head catch up with my heart when it comes to all this."

"I know. And it's okay. You're here. Just the fact that you're willing to endure my sister's irrational ass and my dad's mood swings means more to me than you could ever know."

She grins. "At least your dad likes me."

"Yeah, he does."

"I wonder if he'll still like me tomorrow?"

I'll be surprised if he even recognizes her tomorrow, but I don't say that. Instead, I kiss her cold cheek.

"You're freezing. We should go inside before you catch pneumonia."

She nods, and the two of us walk back toward the house with my dumb, wet beagle right by our side.

chapter nineteen

Brandon

"Lily, I think he's dead."

"He's not dead, Lucy. He's asleep."

"You don't know, he *could* be dead."

I try not to laugh. I'd hate to spoil the fun they're having. Instead, I fake a snore, causing my nieces to explode with giggles.

"See, Lucy! Told ya he wasn't dead. *And* he's smiling. Dead people don't smile."

My eyes snap open, making them both squeal with laughter. In a flash, I wrap my arms around them and throw the blanket over our heads. I'm instantly bombarded with hugs and kisses from the cutest five year olds on the planet.

"Don't tickle us, Uncle B!"

Which of course is a request for tickles, so I do. When they're finally breathless and tired, I kiss each of their cheeks and snuggle them close. Glancing at my watch, I notice it's nearly eight.

I haven't slept this late in years. Feels good.

"You two are up awfully early."

"Mom calls it the butt-crack of dawn," Lily says. "We don't know what that means."

Lucy makes a face. "But it sounds gross."

I laugh. "Yeah, it does. Is your mom awake?"

Lucy nods. "She told us to come wake you up. She's making bacon."

"And eggs," Lily says.

"Sounds delicious. Can I take a shower first?"

They both nod.

"Mom says your girlfriend is here."

"That's right. Her name is Steph."

"Step?"

"*Steph.* With an F sound on the end."

They practice saying it a couple times. It's the cutest thing I've ever seen and makes me love them so much more. It also explains why they still call me Uncle B. *Brandon* was just too impossible for them to pronounce when they were toddlers.

Lily beams brightly. "Let's go wake her up, too!"

The twins are off the bed and out the door before I can even blink.

"Girls, wait!"

I rush next door, only to find Steph's door wide open and my two nieces on each side of her bed, looking at her with wide eyes.

"She's so pretty," Lily whispers to her sister.

"Just like a princess."

It's the first time I've ever watched her sleep. Steph's facial features are relaxed, and the worry lines that tend to always live on her forehead are all but gone.

Beautiful.

Steph must sense she's being watched, because her eyes snap open.

Lucy walks toward the bed. "Hi, Step."

"It's not *Step*," Lily says as she moves closer, too. "It's *Steph*. F sound. 'Member?"

"Wow." Steph sits up in bed and watches as my two very friendly nieces climb up on each side of her. "Good morning, girls. I thought I had double vision there for a second."

The twins giggle.

"I think 'Double Vision' was Foreigner, right? 1980?"

"1978."

I smirk and sit down at the bottom of the bed while Steph turns her attention to the girls who are snuggled very close to her side.

"I don't think your uncle told me that you were twins. He *definitely* didn't tell me you were identical twins."

Oops.

"How can I tell you apart?" Steph asks.

"I'm Lily, and I have this." She points to the mole on her chin.

"And I'm Lucy, and I don't."

Steph nods. "Well, that's very helpful. I'll just look for the mole. Thank you."

It's the first time I've seen Steph interact with kids. The girls bombard her with questions, and she answers them all with a quiet patience that's really amazing to see. Not that I doubted it before, but she's going to make a great teacher. It's just too bad she'll have to deal with middle school or high school students instead of sweet little girls like my nieces.

"Girls, we should let Steph get dressed, and I need to shower. Will you go tell your mom we'll be down in a few minutes?"

"Okay!" They yell in unison before kissing each of Steph's cheeks. I'm kissed next, and as they run out of the room, they're arguing about who gets to sit next to Steph.

"They love you already."

Steph smiles sleepily. "They're sweet girls."

I crawl up the bed. Steph laughs and lies back against the pillow. I hover above her, just barely brushing her chest to mine. Dipping my head, I kiss her gently.

"Good morning."

"Good morning," she says.

"How'd you sleep?"

"Okay. It took me a while to get there. Strange house. New bed."

"You could have come to my room."

"Then we both would have been awake."

"That really wouldn't have bothered me at all."

She grins, and I can't resist kissing her again. And again. Until finally, she whispers my name against my lips.

"Your family is waiting for us," she says softly.

I groan and kiss her one last time before climbing out of bed. I'm nearly to the door when she calls my name.

"I hate to admit it, but those pajamas are pretty sexy."

I slept in an Army T-shirt and camo pants.

"Hmm. There might be hope for you yet."

"Maybe."

I give her a wink before heading back to my room.

Breakfast is madness, but that's not unusual at our house. Christian's cooked a big breakfast, and the girls are excited to be sitting on each side of Steph. My dad, full of energy this morning, is telling us a story he's told a million times about night fishing in a Vietnamese river during his second tour. It amazes me how he can vividly recall an event from forty years ago but can't tell me what we had dinner for last night.

He really can't. I already asked.

We've learned not to point out when Dad's memory gets spotty because it agitates him, and his agitation scares the girls. We've been lucky so far this morning. Christian and I were both thrilled when he recognized Steph and actually called her by name. His good mood and healthy appetite has seemed to relax my sister, and she's actually asked Steph some questions about growing up in Indiana.

Without a doubt, breakfast has been a thousand times more enjoyable than last night's dinner.

"Stephanie, tell us about your parents," Dad says.

Christian's fork clatters against her plate.

"Sorry," she mutters.

I watch as Steph takes a deep breath.

"My mom lives in a little town just outside of Indianapolis. She's the secretary at my old elementary school."

"And your dad?"

Steph glances at the girls. I know she's wondering how much she can say.

My sister clears her throat. "Girls, let's go pick out a movie to watch with Steph."

I smile gratefully at my sister as the three of them head into the living room. Once they're gone, Steph turns toward my dad.

"My dad was killed by friendly fire in Desert Storm," she says.

I can tell by the expression on his face it's the last thing he expected to hear.

"I'm sorry to hear that, Steph."

"Thank you."

"Which branch?"

"Army."

Suddenly, his expression darkens, and I stiffen for the inevitable outburst.

"What's wrong, Dad?"

"I'm just . . . trying to do the math."

Steph switches chairs so that she can sit beside him. "I understand. I hate math, too. What are you trying to figure out?"

"Well, if you're Brandon's age . . . did you even know your father?"

"No, he was killed before I was born."

"Oh."

Dad's face relaxes. So does every muscle in my body.

Steph reaches into her shirt and pulls out her dad's dog tags. She lifts it over her head and hands the chain to my father. He slowly reads the inscription.

"Ah, he was just a kid. That must have been hard on you . . . growing up without him."

"Yes, it was."

Dad gazes thoughtfully at her. "I could sit here and tell you that you should be honored your father died serving his country, but I bet you've heard that a lot. And I bet you hate hearing it."

Steph glances at me, probably looking for a clue as to how to answer him. I just shrug, because I'm clueless. I mean, the morning's going so well. She might as well just be honest.

"It's sometimes hard to hear, yeah."

Suddenly, the girls rush back into the kitchen, each of them grabbing Steph by the hand.

"Come on," Lily says. "The movie's starting without you."

Steph smiles apologetically at Dad, making him laugh as he hands the tags back to her.

"Go on," he says. "We'll talk later."

"You're sitting by me," Lucy says as the three of them head into the living room.

Dad and I both chuckle as they go.

"I like her, Brandon."

"Thank you. I like her, too."

"Smart, too. I don't know how serious you are, but she must be pretty important to you if you've brought her home."

"She's very important to me."

He nods and reaches for another piece of toast. "I figured as much. Have you two had a discussion about what the next four years are going to be like for you?"

"She has a vague understanding, yeah."

"And how does she feel about it?"

"She's . . . not thrilled, to be honest."

"Well, of course she's not. Everything she knows about the military begins and ends with the death of her father. It's a wonder she's dating you at all."

No kidding. I don't dare tell him that Steph and I are in a weird limbo stage. That would just confuse him, especially since I can barely explain it myself.

"Brandon, I wasn't a good husband to your mom. But you know that."

"Dad, we aren't really talking marriage just yet. I'm focused on graduation and AIT. It's far, far too early for us to be talking about wedding vows."

"Maybe, but it's something you should think about. Soldiers sometimes don't make the best spouses. Especially ones who would rather sign up for another tour of duty than come home to a wife who's just chomping at the bit to start a family."

His mental clarity this morning is really starting to scare me.

"Dad, I'm committed to the military. Just like you always wanted."

"Just like I always wanted," he says quietly. "But is it what *you* want?"

It feels like a trap, so I give him my standard response.

"Absolutely, Dad. You know I've always wanted to be like you."

He leans back in his chair and watches me closely.

"You want to be like me?"

"Of course. Always have."

"Brandon, you don't want to be like me. I am an old man, and my memory is fading. Some days are better than others, but that doesn't change the fact that every day, I lose another memory. I forget something that was important to me once upon a time. It's like a drain. The memory just flows out of me and disappears. And once it's gone, it's usually gone for good. But there are other days when I remember *everything*, and that's not good, either."

"Why isn't it good?"

"Because there are some things I wish I could forget."

"Like?"

"Like the fact that I was a bad husband. A bad father."

I shake my head. "I don't think you were a bad father. You were a little strict—"

"I was very strict."

"Okay, very strict. But not bad. I would never say that."

"Maybe not every day. But I was a bad husband. Every single day. Nobody would dispute that. Your mom deserved better. I hope she found it."

"She left *you*."

"Yeah, she did. And I deserved it."

This is getting deep. And very un-Dad like. We don't do this. We don't sit around, talking about his disease and how he was a horrible husband.

"Listen to me, Brandon. While I'm still of fairly sound mind, I want to offer the most important piece of advice I can give you. And I want you to write it down, because you can't trust your memory. I'm living proof of that. Find a pencil."

With a laugh, I get up from the table and hunt for a notepad and pen in one of the drawers.

"This is more important than how to clean your gun. Or how to properly make your bed. Or one of the million other things I taught you when you were a kid. It's the most important thing I could ever, ever teach you."

I sit back down at the table. "Okay, Dad. Let's hear it."

"Ready?"

"Go for it."

"Be a good husband. Be a good father."

My pencil freezes. That's not what I was expecting at all.

"Write it down, son."

I write it down.

"That's what's important in this life. I put the emphasis on the wrong things for far too long. It's not how many push-ups you can do or how fast you can run. It's not how many medals or stripes you earn. It's family. Your wife. Your kids. And then their kids. It has taken sixty years and an incurable memory-robbing disease for me to figure it out, but I finally have. So keep that piece of paper. And someday, when you marry that pretty girl sitting in the living room, read it from time to time. Because I won't be around to remind you of how precious she is."

A lump forms in my throat, because with those words, I finally understand. My father's not just offering words of wisdom to me. He's saying goodbye. Today. While he's still mentally competent enough to do so.

"Dad, it could be years until—"

"And it could be tomorrow. We don't know, Brandon. We never know. We just keep going, hoping for the best, but preparing for the opposite."

"Soldier on," I whisper.

Dad nods. "That's still good advice. Write that down, too."

I don't need to, but I write it down, anyway.

"Brandon, don't be me. Be better than me. Be the man I should have been. That way, when you're old and gray and your memory is shot to hell, you'll have no regrets. Promise me."

"I promise, Dad."

"Good."

After folding up the paper and sticking it in my pocket, I take my dad by the arm and lead him to his recliner. Steph and the twins are sitting on the couch, while Christian's in the rocking chair, reading a magazine.

"Uncle B, do you want to sit with us?" Lily asks.

"I would love to sit with you."

I lift her into my arms and sit down on the couch. She snuggles against my chest and continues watching the movie.

Steph turns to me. "Everything okay?"

I look over at my dad. His eyes are already closed.

"Looks like you wore him out," Steph whispers.

"It was a deep conversation."

"But good?"

"Very good."

Without a doubt, it was the most mature conversation I've ever had with my father. It's just too bad it took us twenty-two years to get here.

But I'm glad we finally made it.

chapter

Twenty

Stephanie

Even though I want to be a teacher, I've never really spent a lot of time around young kids. Lucy and Lily are adorable and fun, but they're also *exhausting*. After a full day of movies, coloring, dancing, and baking, I can't deny I'm thankful I'll be teaching older kids. The girls' constant need to be entertained also has me feeling sympathetic toward Brandon's sister. It's really no wonder she's cranky. Being a single mom, working full-time, and taking care of her dad can't be easy. Despite my newfound compassion for Christian, I still try to avoid her. She's not happy with me, or the fact that I'm here, but she's seemed to accept it and hasn't tried to pick a fight since last night's dinner.

By mid-afternoon, the girls have settled down long enough to take a nap. Brandon and Christian are at the kitchen table, talking in hushed whispers about their dad's care while I keep Mr. Walker company in the living room. I know very little about Alzheimer's and its various stages, but even I can tell that today has been a good day. He ate a big breakfast, a decent lunch, and has stayed alert and lucid throughout the afternoon. I've always heard that routine is important for dementia patients, so I've been a little worried that having a house full of people would agitate him. But so far, it's been a great day. Maybe being around family helps.

He's sitting in his recliner, watching a documentary on the Civil War while I flip through a family photo album. There aren't many pictures, but there are pages of newspaper clippings, including one where Mr. Walker was awarded the Silver Star for rescuing two wounded soldiers during the Battle of Khe Sanh. In the picture, he stands tall and dignified in his uniform. By his side is his wife, Diana, gazing proudly at her husband. It makes me wonder if she was just forcing a smile for the picture or if she was truly happy that he was being recognized for his heroism. And, if she *was* happy, what happened later on to make her throw it all away and leave her family behind?

So many questions.

"You're quiet over there," Mr. Walker says softly.

"I was just looking at this picture of you being awarded the Silver Star."

"That was a good day. September. 19 . . ." his voice trails off as he tries to remember the year. Hoping to help him out, I look closely at the newspaper print.

"I'm not sure. The date has faded on the article."

"It was September 1968. Or was it '69?"

I'm just about to tell him it's okay if he doesn't remember. Anyone would have trouble remembering an event that happened so long ago. But before I can get the words out of my mouth, he quickly leaps to his feet.

"It was 1968. I'm sure it was 1968!"

"Mr. Walker, it's okay—"

"It's not okay!" His breath is ragged as he turns to me. His eyes are cloudy. His expression pained. "Who are you? What are you doing in my house?"

"I'm . . ."

Brandon and Christina run into the living room.

"Who is she? What is she doing here?"

Christian takes her father by the arm. Brandon sprints to my side.

"Dad, that's Steph. She's Brandon's girlfriend."

"Brandon doesn't have a girlfriend! And if he does, he certainly doesn't need one. He should be focused on his drills. Focused on school. Just watch. He'll get her pregnant. Then he won't go to college at all!"

"Dad, he's already in college. Everything is fine. Let's get you to your bedroom."

As Christian leads him to his room, he keeps shouting random insults about what a slut I am and what a failure Brandon is. I don't even realize I'm crying until Brandon wraps me in his arms.

"He doesn't know what he's saying, Steph. I promise he doesn't have a clue."

"I'm so sorry," I whisper.

"You didn't do anything, sweetheart."

"I must have."

"You didn't. I promise."

Brandon pulls me over to the couch. With a sad smile, he gently wipes away my tears with his fingertips.

"He was having such a good day. What did I do?"

"You didn't do anything. This is normal . . . if you can call it that. This is every day. Christian was just telling me she was surprised we'd avoided an outburst. It was only a matter of time. Medication will help calm him down. Tomorrow he won't even remember the things he said. And we never remind him. It just upsets him, and that's the last thing we ever want to do."

"How sad."

"Yeah, it is, but it also makes me grateful for our talk this morning. It was the most stable I've seen him in months. And I know everything he said to me was genuine, despite the garbage he just spewed at us."

"What did he say this morning?"

"He said he was a bad husband and father, and that he didn't teach me what was important in life. He said I need to really think about my future. And if I'm lucky enough to have you in it, I need to always remember how precious you are and to be sure my family is always my number one priority. He told me to remember it, because he won't be around to remind me."

"Wow. That almost sounds like—"

"A goodbye. I know."

I snuggle deeper into his arms.

"I'm glad the girls were napping."

"Me, too." Brandon kisses the top of my hair. "I'm sorry you had to see that. I know it's scary."

It is. And it makes me feel even more compassion for his sister.

A little later, Christian returns to the living room. She doesn't even acknowledge me. Just mutters something about making burgers for dinner before heading toward the kitchen.

"She really hates me."

Brandon lifts my face toward his. "No, she doesn't. But even if she did, it wouldn't matter. I love you."

"I love you, too."

We smile at each other before he leans in, kissing me softly.

Kentucky moonlight shines through the window. It's pretty and bright, making it impossible to sleep. Not that it matters. I never rest well when I'm not in my own bed. The house is cozy and warm, but the sounds and smells make it unfamiliar, and if there's one thing I thrive on, it's familiarity.

I'm a lot like Brandon's dad in that way.

Mr. Walker slept on and off the rest of the evening. The twins didn't even get the chance to say goodbye before their dad picked them up. My guilt was heavy, and I had apologized repeatedly, but Christian and Brandon both assured me I wasn't to blame.

"This is normal," Christian had said.

This is normal. I've heard that a lot over the past few days. As a future English teacher and just a general lover of words, I find it interesting how one phrase can have so many different meanings. To me, this situation is anything but typical. For Brandon's family, today was simply a regular day.

It's hard to imagine, and it makes me sad to try.

Restless and fidgety, I decide a change of scenery is needed. And maybe a glass of warm milk. I crawl out of bed, grab my book out of my bag, and head downstairs.

The house is mostly dark, except for a dim light shining from the kitchen. I manage to make it there without banging into furniture, and I've just opened the refrigerator when I hear someone sniffle quietly. I turn to find Christian sitting at the kitchen table. She's wrapped in a robe and holding a glass of wine.

"Sorry. I didn't realize anyone else was awake."

Christian shrugs. "I'm always awake, it seems."

I nod and reach into the fridge. "I can't sleep. I thought I'd make some warm milk."

"Does that help?"

"Usually, yeah."

"Mom used to make us warm milk when we couldn't sleep," she says. "But it never worked. It just gave me gas."

I laugh softly and reach for a mug. We're both quiet while the milk warms. Once it's ready, I join her at the table.

"Does wine help?"

Christian glances at her glass. "Sometimes. I really just drink it to relax after a long day. At this rate, I'll be an alcoholic by the time I'm thirty."

I don't say anything. I just drink my milk.

"Oh, come on, Steph. That was funny."

I grin. "It was a little funny. I just don't know when it's okay to laugh about . . . all this. I don't want to do or say the wrong thing."

"I understand."

We sit quietly for a few minutes until a loud snore makes me jump.

"Sorry." Christian points toward the baby monitor on the island. "It's the only way I can hear him at night. Dad's bedroom is down here, right beside the living room. Using the stairs isn't such a good idea with his bad coordination. At night, I either have to use the monitor or sleep on the couch, and the couch sucks."

"I think you made a good choice."

She nods and takes another sip of wine.

"My brother loves you. You know that, right?"

I smile. "I do. Brandon's never been shy about how he feels."

"And how do *you* feel?"

"I love him, too. I know you probably don't want to hear that, and I know you don't like me. I just wish I understood why."

She sighs and pours herself another glass.

"When Brandon first told me he was interested in you, I tried to convince him it was a bad idea. It's his last semester, and his focus needs to stay on school. But, according to him, you're even more focused than he is, and his grades are still good, so . . ."

"We're both determined to graduate on time. That's never changed."

"But then he told me how you feel about the military, and while I understand why you feel that way, I can't help but worry that the cycle is repeating."

"What cycle?"

Christian takes a long sip of her wine before continuing. "When I was in high school, I had three goals—make my father proud, become a nurse, and marry Jordan Young. We were the classic high school cliché. He was quarterback of the football team. I was head cheerleader. Once we were engaged, Jordan told me he wanted me to be a wife and mother and nothing else. So, that's what I did. Then we had the girls, and everything was great until I mentioned I was ready to take some college classes and start working on my degree. He refused to support me. Wouldn't even discuss it. I did it anyway."

"Good for you."

"Is it?" Christian shakes her head. "Sometimes I wonder."

"Becoming a nurse was your dream. Your husband should have supported you. I mean, I'm not an expert, but isn't that what relationships are all about?"

"In theory. But in reality, my dream cost me my marriage. And it costs my girls every single day. It's spring break. We should be having a good time. Instead, they are in Lexington with their father, because it's *his week*. So was it really worth it? I don't know." Christian gazes thoughtfully at me. "You see, that's why I was so concerned about Brandon. He fell very hard and very fast for you, and you made it clear you didn't support his dream of becoming a soldier."

I shake my head. "It's not the same thing. I didn't even know he *was* a soldier."

"I know, and it was wrong of him to keep that from you. What happened when you found out?"

"Brandon didn't tell you?"

"Brandon tells me very little. I'm apparently too opinionated."

"Oh. Well, I kicked him out of the apartment."

"And how long did that last?"

"Three days."

The worst three days of my life.

Christian nods. "So now the two of you are in this weird gray area that I'm afraid is going to end exactly like I predicted from the very beginning— with my brother having his heart broken."

I bow my head. She's right. I'm sitting here, passing judgment on her ex-husband. But haven't I done the exact same thing?

"I don't want to break his heart, Christian."

"Just the fact you're here proves that to me. Why else would you be in these mountains on your spring break with a bitchy sister and a forgetful father if you didn't love him? But can you love *all* of him? Every little part of him? Even the part that scares you to death?"

Of course I can. I already do.

"Steph, if you learn anything from this visit, I hope it's this. Plans change. Memories fade. People leave. For every amazing thing that happens to you, there are twenty crappy things just waiting to knock the smile off your face. But you keep smiling. You keep loving. You soldier on, just like Dad says. You find joy wherever you can, and you hold on to it as tightly as possible."

She drains her glass and sets it next to the empty bottle.

"Wow. That was either really profound or I've had way too much wine."

I laugh lightly. "I think a little of both. But that doesn't make your words any less true."

Christian grins and rises from the table.

"I think I'm finally tired enough to sleep, Steph."

"Me, too."

She turns off the light, and the two of us walk upstairs. Her room is the first door on the right.

"Just so you know," I tell her just as she steps inside her room. "I meant what I said. The last thing I want to do is break Brandon's heart."

"Then don't."

She closes the door behind her.

I walk toward my room, but my feet have a mind of their own, and they lead me to Brandon's door. Very quietly, I turn the knob and step inside, pulling the door gently closed behind me. Moonlight streams through his curtains, illuminating his sleeping face, but the light doesn't seem to faze him at all.

Soldiers can sleep anywhere.

Brandon's lying on his back with his arm outstretched, and I try to resist the urge to climb in.

I fail.

Pulling back the blanket, I carefully climb into his bed, snuggling close to his side. His arm automatically wraps around me, pulling me closer. He turns slightly toward me until we're lying face-to-face. Taking a deep breath, I ghost my finger along his dimpled cheek and think about the past few months. I think about how happy I've been, and how Brandon has been a part of every single second of my happiness. He loves me. Every part of me. Even the irrational, selfish part of me that could have ruined it all.

The thought makes me shake uncontrollably.

Brandon's arm tightens around me, and his eyes snap open.

"Steph?" His voice is just a whisper.

"Hi."

"What's wrong?"

"Nothing's wrong."

"Are you cold?"

I don't answer immediately. The truth is, I *was* cold. And bitter. And scared.

"I'm not so cold anymore. I guess I just needed something warm and familiar."

Brandon gazes at me with a sweet, sleepy smile on his face.

"You needed me, Steph."

"I did need you."

"I needed you, too."

He doesn't ask why I'm in his bed, and he doesn't ask me to leave. He just tightens the blanket around us, and then we both close our eyes.

chapter

Twenty-one

Stephanie

It's our last morning in Applewood, and it's the third day that Brandon has skipped his five o'clock run. On the first day, we'd left early to beat the traffic on I-65. The second day we were both awakened by two adorable little girls.

And today . . . well, today is the best morning of all, because we are a tangle of gentle arms and soft blankets. We're awake, but we haven't said a thing.

Our lips are just too busy.

His are sliding down the column of my neck, and the soft moans coming from mine make actual words impossible. Our hands explore places they've never touched. Beneath shirts. Below waists.

Innocent touches in not-so-innocent places, causing us to gasp with pleasure and whimper with need, leaving us shaking and breathless.

And that's with our clothes on.

We smile goofily at each other before dissolving into quiet laughter.

Brandon throws the blanket over our heads and smothers me with kisses. "Good morning."

"Epic understatement."

"And that's with pajamas. Just imagine—"

"That's probably not a good idea."

"Hmm. Probably not." Brandon gently brushes his nose against mine. "Someday, though. Not today, but someday."

"Definitely someday."

It's still early, so we lay and talk for a while. I tell him about my late-night chat with his sister and how we both walked away alive. His smile fades when I mention her ex-husband.

"Jordan's not a bad guy," Brandon says. "He just wasn't good enough for my sister."

"Would any guy really be good enough?"

"Probably not, but he could have tried a little harder. That's what you do when you love somebody."

The alarm on his phone goes off, reminding us we have responsibilities today. Christian has a twelve-hour shift at the hospital. A nurse's aide always stays with Mr. Walker when Christian has to work, but Brandon convinced her to give the nurse the day off.

"We should get downstairs," Brandon says.

He gives me one more toe-curling kiss and heads to the shower. Worried that we're running late, I rush to my room and change out of my pajamas before making my way downstairs. I breathe a sigh of relief when I see Christian standing over the stove.

"Good morning, Christian."

"Good morning. Did the warm milk help?"

The warm bed was better.

"It did. Best night of sleep I've had in weeks."

"Good. Brandon awake?"

"Yeah, he's in the shower."

"Dad's still sleeping . . . or he was the last time I checked. He's usually up by eight. There are some mornings he needs help getting out of bed. Other days, he does just fine on his own. It's a crap shoot, so have Brandon check on him." She glances up at the kitchen clock and sighs heavily. "Dad likes two slices of lightly buttered toast with his eggs and bacon."

"Lightly buttered toast. Got it."

"Good, because this is almost done, and I'm running late. Don't let it burn. It'll just make him cranky."

I take the spatula and quickly flip the bacon.

"Lightly buttered toast. Don't burn the bacon."

"Right. Numbers are on the fridge. Brandon has my cell."

"We'll be fine."

I hope.

She thanks me and tosses a banana in her purse before rushing out the front door.

I finish breakfast, and I'm thrilled not to completely scorch the bacon or burn down the kitchen. Five minutes later, I have Mr. Webster's two slices of lightly buttered toast waiting for him, along with his bacon and eggs. I seem to remember him liking orange juice for breakfast, so I pour a glass and set it next to his plate.

When eight o'clock arrives, I head to Mr. Walker's room to see if he needs any help getting out of bed."

"Mr. Wal—"

I freeze in my tracks when I see that his room is empty.

"Mr. Walker?"

I check everywhere. The downstairs bathroom. Back to the kitchen. I even check the front porch, but there's no sign of him. I'm confident he couldn't have climbed the stairs by himself, so I grab my jacket and rush outside, hoping to find him on the porch.

Nothing.

"Mr. Walker?"

I yell and yell, but the only sound I hear in return is Duke's frantic bark coming from behind the house.

That's when I remember the pond.

My heart races as I run to the back of the house. It might be spring, but the mountain air is still cold and a soft frost gently dusts the ground. In the distance, I can see Duke standing at the edge of the pond.

And I see Brandon's dad sitting on the wooden dock.

Relief floods my veins as I run toward the water. I don't want to frighten him, so I stop just short of the dock. Duke rushes to my side.

"Good boy," I whisper, petting the top of his head.

Slowly, I step up onto the creaky wood. Mr. Walker looks up at me and smiles.

"Good morning, Stephanie."

He knows my name! I sigh with relief.

"Good morning, Mr. Walker. What are you doing out here?"

"Just looking."

"It's pretty cold just to be looking."

"Is it?" He seems surprised. That's when I notice he isn't wearing shoes.

"Mr. Walker, where are your shoes?"

He nods toward the water.

"You threw your shoes in the water?"

"She needed them."

"Who needed them?"

"Diana."

His wife.

"Diana loved to swim."

His legs twitch, and I begin to panic.

I have to get him away from the water. I have to get him back to the house.

"It's too cold to swim today, Mr. Walker."

He nods, but I have no idea if he understands me.

"I was a bad husband, Stephanie. I should have gone swimming with her more."

"That's okay. Diana wouldn't want you to swim today. It's way too cold."

Mr. Walker turns his head toward me.

"My son loves you."

I'm close to tears.

"I know he does. I love him, too."

"He'll take care of you, Stephanie. Will you take care of him?"

"I promise I will."

"And you'll go swimming with him?"

Does Brandon like to swim? I have no idea. But it doesn't matter right now.

"Yes, Mr. Walker. When the weather is warmer, I'll be sure to go swimming with him."

He seems satisfied with that answer as he gazes down into the water. I hear footsteps behind us. I know it's Brandon, but I don't dare turn around.

"Mr. Walker, I'm very cold. Would you take me back to the house?"

He tilts his head to the side. "Are you cold, Stephanie?"

My teeth chatter in response, but I know it's not from the chill in the air.

"Yes, I am."

"Well, then, we need to get you inside. Wouldn't want you to catch a cold."

He steps away from the edge of the dock and turns toward the house. I take his left arm, and it's only then that I let myself look at Brandon. His face is pale, and his eyes are filled with tears.

"Good morning, Brandon. We need to get Stephanie inside. She's cold."

I watch as Brandon takes a long, steadying breath.

"Okay, Dad. Let's take her inside."

Brandon moves closer to his dad and takes his arm, and the three of us walk back toward the house.

The house is too quiet. It unnerves me. A house this beautiful and big should have happy sounds and sweet smells, and it probably does when the girls are home. But today it's too silent. Too still.

Time passes slowly when you're waiting, and with each ticking of the clock, I grow a little more anxious. I've tried to keep busy. I've thrown out the cold breakfast, done the dishes, and mopped the floor. There's nothing left to clean, unless I want to go upstairs and strip the beds.

I don't.

Instead, I sit at the kitchen table and try to read the newspaper, but the words swim on the page. Duke refuses to leave my side, and I'm grateful for the company. Brandon is with his dad, and they, along with Christian and Dr. Edsall, are in the bedroom. They've been in there for over an hour. I have no idea what's going on, but I don't need a doctor's diagnosis to know that Mr. Walker had a hallucination of his wife swimming in the pond.

And he was ready to swim with her.

My mind swirls with what ifs... conjuring image after horrifying image of what could have happened today.

I can't stop shaking, despite the blanket that surrounds me.

Suddenly, I hear a door open, and seconds later, Brandon walks into the kitchen.

"Hey," he says softly.

As soon as I hear his voice, I fall apart.

Brandon lifts me into his arms and carries me into the living room. Once we're on the couch, I bury my face against his chest. I shake. I cry. He rocks me and murmurs sweet words that just make me cry harder.

"I'm sorry. I don't want you to see me this way. I should be stronger. I want to prove to you I can handle this."

"Sweetheart, you don't have to prove anything to me."

"I do. I absolutely do. Because this is *our* life now. This is *our* normal, and I want you to know that you can depend on me."

"Steph, look at me."

I lift my eyes toward his.

"You saved my father's life today. If you hadn't . . ."

His entire body begins to tremble, and I wrap my arms around him so the blanket covers us both.

"You saved him," Brandon whispers, resting his forehead against mine. "You were so good with him. You knew exactly what to say. I couldn't have done that. I couldn't have stayed calm and collected. *You* did. You saved his life."

I shake my head. "We don't know if he would have jumped."

"We don't know that he wouldn't have." Brandon gently wipes my cheek. "Thank God we didn't find out."

We hold each other close. I have no idea how long we stay like that, but eventually, the bedroom door opens, and I open my eyes to find Christian and the doctor watching us closely.

"Brandon, I think Dr. Edsall should take a look at Steph."

I wipe at my face. "No, I'm okay. Honestly. I just needed a good cry."

"I could at least check your blood pressure?" Dr. Edsall offers. "I think it would make Christian feel a lot better."

"I'd feel better, too," Brandon says. "Let the doctor check you out, Steph."

"Only if you let her check you out, too."

He chuckles and shakes his head. "Always so stubborn. Okay."

Dr. Edsall checks our vitals. Both our blood pressures are elevated, which doesn't surprise anyone. I refuse the light sedative she offers, so she prescribes a hot bath, a favorite book, and a good night's sleep.

After Christian walks the doctor to the door, she returns to the living room and sits down right beside us. I'm still in Brandon's lap. I'm warm here.

"How are you really?"

"I'm okay."

She nods and reaches for my hand. "Steph, I want to thank you."

"Please don't thank me. I didn't—"

"Don't say you didn't do anything. You probably saved our father from drowning. He honestly believed our mom was in the pond, and I firmly believe if you hadn't found him, he would have jumped in. Even if he had survived the fall, he wouldn't have survived the cold temperature, and he certainly wouldn't have survived the water."

"Are the hallucinations new?" Brandon asks.

"He's only had one other that I'm aware of. It was of Mom, too. He thought he saw her sitting in the porch swing. Dr. Edsall thinks he's harboring some deep remorse for the way he treated her. It's just waited until now to manifest itself."

Brandon nods. "He's talked about her a lot the past three days. That's unusual."

"I mentioned that to the doctor. She thinks it's because of the disruption of his routine. You're here. The girls aren't. And he met Steph. Dad recognized pretty quickly that the two of you are close. Maybe it's reminded of him when he and Mom were young and in love. Maybe it's a complete coincidence. We have no way of knowing."

"Is he sleeping now?" I ask.

"Yeah. He was very relaxed during the doctor's exam, and I know that's because of you. Brandon told me how patient and calm you were. How you convinced him to come inside. I'm a nurse, and I don't know if I could have handled it as well."

"Well, I'm a mess now."

She laughs softly. "You know what? You've earned the right to be a mess. Things happen at the hospital that really shake me up sometimes, but I manage to hold it together until I'm in my car. There are many times I cry all the way home. I am not Wonder Woman, and neither are you. It's okay to be human."

And then the most amazing thing happens.
She hugs me.

It's late in the afternoon when we finally get packed and head downstairs. We'd only planned to stay a few days, but I can tell Brandon's disappointed to be going home so soon. He didn't get to see much of his nieces, and he never got the chance to show me his hometown.

I promised we'd come back, right after graduation.

This afternoon, Brandon added extra locks to the doors while Christian arranged for a nurse's aide to be there day and night. It will be expensive, but hopefully it'll take some stress off Christian so that she can have a life of her own and keep Mr. Walker safe and comfortable at the same time.

Saying goodbye to Mr. Walker was hard. Maybe it was because I never had a dad of my own, or maybe it was because I was still emotional from what happened at the pond, but when he hugged me, I cried like a baby. This made him nervous until I promised they were happy tears.

And they were. Nothing but happy.

While Brandon and Christian make some final arrangements in the kitchen, I walk around the living room, looking at the pictures on the wall. I stop when I come across a photo of Mr. Walker in his uniform, with an American flag in the background.

It looks so much like the picture of my dad.

Reaching down into my shirt, I pull out the ball chain and my dad's tags. I let the silver slide through my fingers as I think about the last few days.

I've spent my life hating the military. In my mind, it had stripped me of the privilege of ever knowing my father. But really, I was angry at the wrong thing, and for the wrong reasons. My dad made a choice, and if his picture is any indication, he was proud of that choice. Just like this picture of Brandon's father. He looks just as proud in this old eight-by-ten as he does in the faded newspaper clipping.

Brandon made his choice, too.

And just like my mother, I have my own choice to make.

I place a kiss on the silver tags and let them fall against my chest.

Suddenly, a set of strong arms wrap around me.

"Hey, sweetheart. Are you ready?"

I twist around and smile into the eyes of my soldier.

My soldier.

And that's when I realize I have no choice at all.

"I'm ready."

chapter
Twenty-Two

Brandon

April arrives, and with it, Steph and I return to our *like-two-ships-passing-in-the-night* routine. I still have a job, thanks to Ms. Linda having sympathy for my lovesick ass, so I've been picking up extra shifts when I can. That, combined with her job and our classes, keeps us apart more than we're together. However, we've continued waking up in each other's arms every morning, which makes the hours apart somewhat bearable but still ridiculously miserable.

I just want to touch her all the time. *Is that so wrong?*

I ask Xavier that exact question at the coffee shop one sunny afternoon. He's stopped by to pick up a muffin for Tessa, who has the flu, which explains why she's buying muffins instead of baking them. I take a break and follow him over to a booth.

"Umm, I sort of assumed you two were already . . . touching."

"Well, we *touch*, of course. You know what I mean."

"But you want to touch more?"

"I want to touch a lot more."

He smirks.

"But there's an issue."

"She loves you. You love her. There is no issue."

"Yes, there is. After graduation, I'll get a short leave before I'm off to Georgia for twelve weeks. I will not sleep with her and then leave her for three months. I love her too much to do that to her. Or to me."

"Can't she go to Georgia with you?"

"No. I have to live in the barracks. Besides, she's going to be looking for a teaching job. I don't expect her to put her life on hold for me, especially when we don't know where my duty station will be until near the end of training."

Xavier nods. "Have you two talked about what you'll do? I mean, is she going with you?"

"We . . . haven't really talked about that."

"Then you're right. You do have an issue."

"Thanks a lot, Xavier."

He chuckles and shakes his head. "Listen, man, if this were any other girl, I'd say go for it and don't worry about the consequences. But this is Steph, and you love her, so the two of you need to have a serious conversation about the future. You *do* see her in your future, don't you?"

"I see her in mine, yeah."

"But?"

"I don't know if she sees me in hers."

"Don't you think it's time to find out?"

Thanks to a late night study group, it's after eleven by the time Steph finally makes it home. She laughs when she sees me sitting on the couch with Bangle in my lap.

"Well, this is a surprise."

"The fact that I'm actually awake? Or that your cat is being friendly to me?"

"Both, to be honest."

Steph walks toward me, and I all but toss her cat aside so she can climb into my lap. Her chest presses against mine, and I let my fingers slide along her back as we hold each other. This position is so, so dangerous, but that doesn't stop me from pulling her tighter against me and kissing her until we're out of breath.

She opens her eyes. "Wow. Hi."

"Hey."

"Something on your mind, Mr. Walker?"

"You."

"Me?"

"Always you."

This makes her smile.

"We need to talk, Steph."

Her face falls.

"It's not bad, I promise."

She doesn't look convinced, so I kiss the tip of her nose.

"I promise."

"Sounds serious. Should I get out of your lap?"

No.

"Probably," I mutter.

Steph laughs and slides onto the couch.

"We need to have a serious conversation about the future," I tell her.

"Okay . . ."

"I want you in mine."

"You do?"

I roll my eyes. "This can't possibly be news to you."

"It's still nice to hear."

"Yeah."

I swallow nervously.

"Brandon?"

"Yeah?"

"I want you in my future, too."

I can't hide my stupid grin.

"We probably do need to talk about it, though," she says. "The logistics and all that."

"Okay, let's talk about it."

We spend the next few minutes discussing AIT and how she can't go with me.

"But I can go with you *after* AIT?"

"Depending on my duty station, yes. We could live in the same town."

"But we couldn't live together?"

"No. Single soldiers have to live on post until they become an E6."

"How long does that take?"

"Up to eight years, and I don't plan on being in the service that long."

She laughs, and then the room grows deathly quiet.

"Wait, you said *single* soldiers."

"Right."

I can hear the wheels grinding. They're *loud*. Or maybe that's my heartbeat. Hard to tell.

"So if we were married . . ."

I take a deep breath. "If we were married, we could live on or off base. Together."

"*If* we're married."

"Yes."

Steph reaches for my hand and slides her fingers along mine.

"Brandon, are you proposing?"

Am I? That really wasn't my intention. Not tonight, anyway.

But I could.

And I would.

But would she want me to?

I love her. It's never been a question. We're young, but we're also old enough to know what we want out of life. We're both driven and have goals we want to accomplish. Family is important to us, and it's easy to imagine having one with Steph someday.

But not today. Even I know we aren't ready for that.

"I love you, Steph."

"I love you, too."

"But I don't think we're ready. Not yet."

Her shoulders visibly relax. "Neither do I."

I grin. *I know my girl so well.*

She wraps her arms around my neck. "There's just so much we don't know, Brandon. Where you'll be. Where *I'll* be. What we'll be doing."

"I know. And you want to teach. You've worked way too hard to give that up, and I'd never ask you to."

"But if I find a teaching job in Indiana, while you're in Georgia . . ."

Steph's looking at me with her big brown eyes, looking for answers I just don't have. If she finds a teaching job while I'm at AIT, she will be tied to that particular school—and that particular town—for the school year. I have no idea where I'll be stationed after training is complete. It would be unfair and selfish of me to ask her to *wait* . . . to just wait and see where I end up and *then* apply to schools in the area. Even if I did ask, and she agreed, there would be no guarantee she could even find a job there.

We have to be smart. We've worked too hard not to be.

"Steph, what was your plan for after graduation?"

She sighs. "Well, I planned to apply for teaching licenses in Indiana, Illinois, and Kentucky. I'll be certified in all three states. I just want to stay as close to Mom as possible."

"I understand. And I agree. I think you should do exactly what you planned."

"But what if . . ."

Her voice trails off, but she doesn't have to finish the thought. I know exactly what she's going to say.

"Steph, I won't ask you to wait."

"Maybe I *want* to wait. Once we know where you'll be on a permanent basis—"

I shake my head. "After AIT, I could be anywhere, and maybe I'll be stationed in some places you don't need to be. Or *can't* be."

"Or you could be stationed close by. You're assuming the worst, Brandon."

"No, I'm *preparing* for the worst. I can't control any of it, but I have to be ready to live with whatever happens. That's the choice I made, Steph, and I'm sorry my choice affects us. I'm sorry it affects you."

With a quiet sigh, Steph crawls back into my lap. She places a soft kiss against the corners of my mouth.

"I'm not sorry, Brandon."

"You're not?"

She shakes her head. "Nope. I love you, and I've decided we're going to be okay, no matter what."

"You've decided, huh?"

"That's right."

"How can you be so sure?"

"Because of something your dad and sister said."

"What did they say?"

"Christian said that for every amazing thing that happens to us, there are other crappy things just waiting to knock the smiles off our faces. But we keep smiling. We soldier on."

I can't deny I'm impressed with my sister's logic.

"And what did my dad say?"

"He said you had promised to take care of me, and that morning at the pond, I promised him I would take care of you. That's why I know we're going to be okay. Both of us are too stubborn not to keep our promises."

"But what about the Army? Are you sure you can handle the fact that I'm a soldier?"

"I can. I don't have a choice."

"You always have a choice, Steph."

Steph sighs softly before placing a soft kiss below my ear.

"That's the thing, Brandon. I don't have a choice at all. I love you. You love me. The only choice we have is to make it work."

I bury my hands in her hair and pull her face to mine. Our hands roam as we kiss, causing shivers to radiate up my spine. Steph breaks the kiss to find the hem of my shirt. She lifts it over my head and tosses it aside.

Then she surprises me by placing her hand over my heart.

"No matter where you are, I will be right *here*."

She lowers her head and places a kiss there.

"But I'm selfish, Steph. I want you in my arms, too. In my bed. In my life. Every single day."

"We'll make it work. We will figure it out."

I kiss her forehead.

"There's . . . something else we need to discuss."

"What's that?"

"Our sleeping arrangements."

"Are you unhappy with your accommodations, Mr. Walker?"

"No, I love them, and that's why we need to talk about it."

With a sigh, Steph slides onto the couch once again. Probably wise. It might be difficult to have a serious conversation about sex with her sitting in my lap.

"We're tempting fate," Steph says. "I know that. Every morning, when we wake up together and do . . . the things we do, I know it's just a matter of time before I'll want more. And you'll want more."

"We're twenty-two years old and in love. I'm pretty sure we already want more."

She smirks, and I see a faint blush creep across her cheeks.

Beautiful.

"I have a confession," she says softly. "You'll be my first."

I can't say I'm shocked, but I am a little surprised. And it makes me thankful that we've waited. Steph doesn't ask, so I don't tell her I haven't exactly been a saint when it comes to girls. I dated a lot in high school, but once I got to college, most girls just wanted to hook-up because of my uniform. That was fun during my first two years of school, but once I became serious about ROTC, I had weekend volunteer missions and morning training sessions, all of which left very little time for girls.

Steph mistakes my silence, and her face falls.

"You're disappointed," she whispers.

"What? No! I'm glad, actually. And a little amazed."

Steph shrugs. "There's nothing amazing about it. I've just never dated much. School was always my focus. Love didn't interest me. Random hook-ups *definitely* didn't interest me, and in college, that's what most guys want."

"Not this guy. He just wants you."

She smiles. "I know. That's another reason why I love him. I also think that's why we should wait to have sex. I just think . . . your leaving is going to be hard enough. Until you're settled—"

"Until *we're* settled."

She nods. "Until we're settled, I just think we should wait. No matter how much I really don't want to."

"I don't want to, either, but I think you're right." I take her hand and gently lace her fingers with mine. "So, what about that *tempting fate* thing? Do you want me to sleep in my room from now on?"

"No. Do you want to?"

"Not really."

With a sweet smile, Steph stands up and pulls me by the hand, leading me down the hallway. We reach her bedroom, and she disappears into the bathroom while I change out of my clothes. After turning off the light, I set the alarm on my phone and climb under the covers. I try to stay awake while she showers, but I must doze off because, suddenly, I'm awakened by the scent of peaches and cream.

"Sleepy head," she whispers against my ear.

I sigh contently as she snuggles into my arms.

"Brandon?"

"Yeah?"

"Speaking of temptation," she says softly, "I'm glad you didn't propose tonight. I would have been tempted to say yes."

Pulling her close, I bury my nose in her hair.

"I would have wanted you to," I whisper.

We hold each other a little tighter before we both drift off to sleep.

chapter

Twenty-Three

Stephanie

The next morning, I head over to Tessa's apartment, armed with orange juice and blueberry muffins from the coffee shop. Finding out from my boyfriend that Tessa has the flu just proves I've seriously neglected my best friend for far too long.

It takes four knocks, but Tessa finally opens the door. When she does, I'm struck by how *green* she looks.

"Wow, you really look terrible."

She sniffles softly. "Did you come over here just to tell me I look like crap? Because trust me, I know."

Smiling apologetically, I dangle the box of muffins in her face. Unfortunately, this causes her eyes to grow wide and sends her running for the bathroom.

Not the effect I was hoping for.

I let myself in and close the door behind me. Xavier's nowhere to be found, so I put the muffins on the table and the juice in the fridge before heading toward her bathroom.

I wait until I hear the flush before knocking on the door.

"You okay in there?"

"No."

"What can I do?"

"You can get in here."

I'm not entirely sure I want to, but she's my best friend, so I slowly open the door. When I peek inside, I find her sitting on the edge of her tub. Her head is bowed as she quietly sobs.

"Tessa?"

She looks up with red-rimmed eyes.

"Tessa, what is it?"

She wipes her eyes and stands up. With a heavy sigh, she opens the drawer under the sink before sitting back down on the tub.

I look down. Five pregnancy tests are lined up in a neat little row.

"Are those . . . what I think they are?"

"Yes."

"Have they been used?"

She nods.

"By *you*?"

"No, Steph, by Xavier. I must say, his aim has been a little off, but—"

"Okay! I'm sorry. It was a stupid question." I sit down, wrapping my arm around her. "You don't have the flu, do you?"

Tessa shakes her head. "I have thrown up every morning for the past week. I was so sure it was the flu, but then I looked at a calendar . . ."

"Oh, Tessa."

This makes her cry harder.

"I just don't understand how it happened, Steph! I mean, I know everybody says that, but I *really* don't get it. I'm on the pill. Xavier *always* uses protection. We've always, always been so careful and responsible."

"What's Xavier saying?"

"I haven't told him. I wanted to take one more test . . . just to be sure. Every morning for the past five mornings . . ."

I look toward the drawer.

Peeing on five different sticks might have been a tad bit excessive.

I don't say that, though. I just wrap my arms around her and hug her tight.

"What am I going to do, Steph?"

"I really think that's a conversation you need to have with Xavier."

"All Xavier thinks about is basketball. He wants to coach somewhere. Anywhere. And I was fine with that because I can cook anywhere. But now . . ." her voice trails off as she points to her stomach. "*This* was not in our plans."

I smile and think about Brandon and his family.

"Tessa, if I've learned anything this semester, it's that plans change. And sometimes, it's not so bad when they do. It makes you grow up. It makes you view the world with completely different eyes.

And you realize the things that seemed so important aren't really important at all."

Her eyes search mine. "Holy crap."

"What?"

"Tell me you're still a virgin."

I blink. "Umm . . ."

"Please tell me you're still a virgin!"

"I'm still a virgin! What is wrong with you?"

Her entire body relaxes. "Really?"

"Yes."

"Good. You've just been so smart, Steph. So responsible. You've kept your focus on school and you'll graduate with honors and get a great teaching job somewhere. I know you love Brandon. I know you do. Please don't be stupid like I've been."

I'm instantly reminded of last night's talk with Brandon. If I'm being honest, I have to admit I'm grateful he initiated the conversation. We've been tempting fate, and it was only a matter of time before our early morning make-out sessions turned into something more. And I wouldn't have regretted it, because I love him. But as I look into the frightened eyes of my best friend, I can't help but feel relieved that Brandon and I are on the same page when it comes to having sex. We both know the timing is crap, and if I was to get pregnant just as he was leaving, I don't know how I would handle that.

I brush Tessa's hair out of her eyes. "Okay, first of all, you are not stupid. You guys have been together a long time, and you love each other. Also, it's not like you're some teenager who just found out she's knocked up. You are a smart, strong, twenty-two-year-old woman who is absolutely capable of being a mother."

Tessa's eyes fill with tears again. "I am?"

"Of course you are. Aren't you happy? Just a little bit?"

Tessa reaches for a tissue and dabs her eyes. "I . . . don't know. I feel a thousand different things. I'm scared. I'm excited. I'm *sick*. I'm mortified. His parents love me, Steph. Like really, really love me. Will this change their opinion of me?"

"Well, if it does, it better change their opinion of their son, too. You didn't make this baby on your own."

"And what about *my* parents? Do you have any idea how many mother-daughter talks I've had to sit through about this very subject? How many times I've listened to my mom tell me that good, Catholic girls remain virgins until their wedding night?" She stops to take a deep breath. "I haven't been a good, Catholic girl in a long time. With all that weighing on me, am I even *allowed* to be a little happy about this?"

"I think you are. I know the timing isn't the greatest, but *this* was happening eventually, right? You guys were planning on getting married and having a family someday."

"But not *now*. Did I tell you about my Aunt Nadia? The one who lives in Chicago?"

I shake my head.

"She owns a gourmet Mexican restaurant. She invited me to work with her chef as soon as I graduate. He's ready to retire but wants to make sure he's leaving his kitchen in capable hands. He would train me, Steph."

"What about Xavier?"

"Xavier's all for it. He's checking out their local high schools and colleges, hoping to find a coaching job. A few are interested."

"Tessa, that's amazing!"

Her face falls. "Is it? I'm just not sure now. And I know there are options out there . . . for unplanned babies. But those aren't options for me. This is *our* baby. It doesn't matter if the timing is right for us. For whatever reason, God has decided this *is* the time. I have to accept that and figure out a way to make it work."

"And you *can* make it work. Women have been making it work for centuries."

She sighs heavily and makes a sour face.

"I need to brush my teeth."

"You do that. I'll get us some juice and meet you in the kitchen."

"Okay."

As I make my way to the fridge, I find it funny how our roles have changed. It's strange, Tessa being so pessimistic while I'm the one busting out the pom-poms. I've never been a silver-lining type of girl. I've never bought into the whole *everything happens for a reason* concept because everything that happened to me seemed crappy and unfair.

Or at least that's what I thought.

But now, I think maybe there is some truth to it. Maybe there is some cosmic reason for things happening just as they do. I didn't go looking for Brandon. He found me, in the most unlikely of places. And because he did, I've been forced to question the enormous chip that has lived on my shoulder for far too long. Brandon was not in my grand plan, just like this baby wasn't in Tessa's, but that doesn't mean they shouldn't be there, and it doesn't mean they can't be wonderful.

Scary, but wonderful.

I sit down at the table just as Tessa comes into the kitchen.

"I left the muffins on the counter. I figure if the scent is enough to make you hurl, it's best to keep them out of sight."

She nods and takes the seat beside me. I watch as she carefully sips her juice.

"I have so much to do," she says.

"You do, but I think you should just take one thing at a time. You have nine months to figure it all out. Right now, your first priority—"

"I have to figure out a way to tell Xavier."

"Yep."

Suddenly, her face brightens. "I can use food!"

"Food?"

"Remember when Becky told Uncle Jesse she was pregnant? She made baby shrimp, baby corn . . ."

I grin. Leave it to my crazy best friend to pull a *Full House* reference out of thin air.

"Xavier loves your *baby* back ribs."

"I know, right?" She excitedly jumps out of her chair and heads to her pantry. "I didn't really plan on grocery shopping today, but—"

"Plans change, Tessa."

She turns toward me with a hopeful expression on her face.

"They do, don't they?"

I walk over and hug her tight.

"They really do."

After a whirlwind trip to the grocery store, I drop Tessa back at her apartment. I left her with her grandmother's recipe book in hand and a massive grin on her face as she began to prepare her baby-themed dinner for Xavier.

I pray Xavier takes the news well. I'd hate to have to kick his ass.

It's a pretty day, and I am a ball of nervous energy for my best friend, so I decide to take a walk around campus. The wind has picked up, so I grab Brandon's hat out of my backseat and use my rearview mirror to make sure it looks right.

I smile at my reflection.

I really love his hat.

Despite the breeze, the sun is nice and warm as I begin my walk. Peyton College is beautiful in the springtime. Students hang out on the quad, kicking around soccer balls and listening to music. Excitement is in the air, filled with the promise of sunshine and, for many of us, graduation. I've spent four years at Peyton College. There are many buildings I've never stepped into and thousands of students I've never met. And that's okay.

I'm ready to move on. I'm ready to start my life.

By this time, I thought I'd know exactly what that meant. I would know where I was headed and what was waiting for me. Mom said she wanted me to be adventurous this last semester, and in a weird way, that's exactly what I'm doing.

I'm jumping headfirst into life without a solid plan.

That's a big deal for a control freak like me.

I look off in the distance and realize there's one last thing I need to do before graduation. It's something I've wanted to do since I was a freshman, but I kept putting it off. Waiting for the right time.

And the right person.

Inevitably, I end up at the coffee shop. I watch Brandon through the window while he waits on a customer. Dressed in his paisley apron, his smile lights up the room, and I can't help but laugh as the little girl on the other side of the counter points at his apron and giggles. When they leave, he sees me through the glass.

I smile and wave.

He waves back just as an older woman, with pretty silver hair and a matching paisley apron walks up behind him, patting him on the back. I can only assume that's Ms. Linda, his manager.

A few minutes later, Brandon walks out into the April sunshine.

"Hey, you."

"Hey, you."

"Nice hat."

I smirk. "You love it?"

"You have no idea."

He steps closer and dips his head, kissing me gently.

"Brandon, will you take a walk with me?"

"I'd love to take a walk with you."

We take each other's hand, and I lead him down the sidewalk and toward the trail that will take us to Rainbow Rock.

chapter

Twenty-four

Brandon

"I wonder where they are now?"

I know it's a rhetorical question, so I don't bother answering.

We're sitting on top of the mountain, overlooking campus. Steph slides her fingers along the multi-colored ink on the gray slab of rock.

"And these people . . . the ones with hearts drawn around their names. Do you think they're still together?"

"Honestly? Probably not."

She frowns. "That's not very optimistic, Brandon."

"No, but it's realistic. Look at the dates. Some of them are more than twenty years old. Do you really think all these people are still in love?"

"I'd like to think so. Rainbow Rock should be something sacred."

"You're right. It should be."

"Have you signed it?"

I shake my head.

"I always meant to," Steph says. "I just kept putting it off. I realized today that I've put it off long enough. We'll start packing soon. Finals are coming up. Chances are good I would have forgotten all about it."

"I'm glad you thought of it. I would have forgotten, too."

Steph excitedly digs into her backpack and pulls out permanent markers in several different colors.

"Pick a shade. Any shade."

"You choose."

"Hmm." She settles on a bright green. "It's not camo, but it'll do."

I chuckle and watch as Steph searches for a bare spot on the gray slab to write our names. She's really starting to embrace this whole soldier situation. Today, she's even wearing my fatigue cap that she apparently stole out of my truck.

Not that I mind. I love when she wears it.

"I'm not an artist, but I think it looks okay," she says as she draws a heart around our names. "Here. You date it."

I take the marker, and just below our names, I write today's date.

"It's perfect, Steph."

She laughs and searches for her phone in her backpack. After snapping a picture of our names on the rock, she then scoots closer and takes a photo of the two of us.

"For Mom," she says.

I smile and lean back against the stone, stretching my legs. Steph rests her head in my lap while I play with her hair that peeks out from under the hat.

"I saw Tessa this morning. She doesn't have the flu," she says.

"Oh?"

"She's pregnant."

I blink. "The flu would be better."

Steph gazes up at me. "You really think so?"

"Right now? Yes, I do."

She nods. "Me, too. They were careful, but it happened anyway. She's so scared, Brandon. Afraid of what her family will say. What *his* family will say. What this means for their future. Xavier doesn't know. She's telling him tonight."

Steph grows quiet, and for a minute, I try to imagine how I'd react if she told me she was pregnant. Would I be happy? Would I say the right things? *Do* the right things?

We just had our conversation about sex last night. And today, we've been given definite proof that our decision to wait is a good one.

"What are you thinking?" she asks quietly.

"Wondering how I'd react if you told me you were having my baby. And thinking it's ironic that you and I just talked about this last night."

"I know. I was thinking that, too. I can't imagine it. I mean, they've been together for two years, and she's still freaking out. We've only known each other a few months."

"We're doing the right thing, Steph."

"I know." She rises up and crawls into my lap, wrapping her arms around my neck. "But someday . . ."

I pull her close. "Someday?"

"We're talking *fireworks*."

"Especially if you're wearing this hat."

"You really love this hat, don't you?"

"I love it on you."

She kisses me, tender and soft, and I can't help but wonder how I got so lucky. We have no idea what our future holds, and I don't have a thing to offer her except a pretty Kentucky house and a loud, barking beagle.

But she loves me anyway.

"Speaking of things I need to do before graduation, what are you doing Sunday?"

"Just studying. What do you want to do?"

I adjust the cap on her pretty head.

"I need to say goodbye to a friend," I tell her.

On Sunday afternoon, we make the drive to Magnolia Gardens. Sunday is typically a day for families, but I know Tom has no family. Or at least none that ever visit.

As we drive to the nursing home, I tell her all about Tom McBride. The two tours in Vietnam. The grenade attack. His blindness. And I tell her about his wife, Connie. By the time we reach the entrance,

Steph is a sobbing mess, and we have to sit in the car another fifteen minutes until she's calm enough to go inside.

I sign us in, and the nurse points us toward the back deck. Like always, Tom is sitting on his bench, his face raised toward the sunshine.

"Good afternoon, Tom."

He turns toward the sound of my voice.

"Afternoon, Brandon." Tom inhales deeply. "Hmm. Either you're smelling particularly good today or you've brought someone to meet me."

I chuckle. "I did bring someone with me. This is Stephanie."

"Your girl?"

"Yes, sir."

He smiles brightly and slides down the bench. Steph and I sit down next to him.

"It's nice to meet you, Mr. McBride."

"You can call me Tom."

"Well, then, you can call me Steph."

"You sound like a Steph," he says with a nod. "And you sound like a sweet girl. I hope Brandon's being good to you."

"He's very good to me."

"I'm glad. There's nothing like being in love. It makes you look at the world differently, don't you think?"

Steph squeezes my hand. "It absolutely does, yeah."

Tom tilts his head in her direction. "I hope you don't mind, but Brandon told me about your father. I'd like to thank you for his service, but I know that doesn't take the pain away. I'm sorry about that."

"Thank you. If his pictures are any indication, he was very proud to serve."

"I'm sure he was. It's a calling, just like with anything else. It's not for everyone, and that's not necessarily a bad thing. What's your calling? Are you in school?"

"I am. I graduate in May. I'm going to be an English teacher."

"Oh? I was a teacher."

For the next hour, Tom and Steph talk about everything from unruly students to Indiana basketball. He avoids talking about his military career, which seems odd since that's typically all he and I discuss when I visit. But I know he's doing it out of respect for Steph. Who knows? Maybe he's grateful to talk about something different, too.

"Brandon, you're very quiet this afternoon."

"Just letting you two talk."

"Well, she's fun to talk to."

"I know she is."

Steph rolls her eyes at the two of us and stands up from the bench. "Well, *she* is going to let you guys do the talking while she looks for a restroom."

I reach up and squeeze her hand. "It's near the entrance. Want me to show you the way?"

"No, stay here and talk to your friend. I'll be right back."

Steph leans down and kisses me before heading inside. I bet she isn't looking for the bathroom at all. She probably just wanted to give us the chance to say our goodbyes.

"She's a bright and beautiful girl," Tom says.

"Yes, she . . .wait a second. How do you know she's beautiful?"

He laughs. "I don't need eyes to see how beautiful she is, Brandon. That girl has a sweet soul. You remember what I said last time you were here?"

"*Love. Honesty. Respect.* I remember."

"And you're doing all those things?"

"Yes, sir."

"Good. Keep doing them. It'll make you better in every way. A better solider. A better man." Tom lifts his head toward the sun and smiles. "But you're not here for a lecture, are you? You're here to tell me goodbye."

I try to swallow the lump in my throat. It's impossible.

"We're graduating soon. I was afraid I might not get another chance to come visit."

"And then you're off to AIT?"

"Yes. Signal Corps training for twelve weeks."

"Well, your girl is here. I guess that means she's accepted you, camouflage and all."

I smile. "She has."

"I'm glad to hear that."

This goodbye is harder than the one with my father. At least I plan on seeing my dad again. The chances of seeing Tom McBride are slim. I can promise to write or call, but we both know it could be difficult, depending on where I'm stationed. Plus, he's not the healthiest man. We both know that. We just don't discuss it.

"I sense you're feeling some guilt, Brandon."

I close my eyes. *How does he know?*

"A little, yes."

"Because I'm an old man with no family?"

Yes.

"Son, I don't want you to worry about me. The doctors and nurses take good care of me. I'd love a Christmas card. Maybe a phone call if you can. But I don't expect it. You forget I was a soldier, too. I know things are different now, as far as technology and all that, but I can't use any of it. And who knows where you'll be? So, if you *can* call, I know you will. But don't feel obligated, and don't feel guilty if you can't. You've been a good friend, Brandon. You've listened to an old man talk about the war and his wife, and you've done it all without falling asleep once."

I laugh.

"I've enjoyed our talks, Tom. You don't know how much."

"Sure, I do. You visited almost every weekend. That's more visits than some of the other guys get, and they have kids who live close by. Plus, you brought Steph to meet me. That shows me our time has been as special to you as it has been to me. I appreciate that."

"It has been. I really . . . don't know when I'll get back to Indiana."

"I know that, too. That's why I said call if you can. Heck, you can even write me a letter. It'll give me the chance to hear a nurse's voice say something to me besides, 'Time for your medication, Mr. McBride.' It'll be a nice change of pace."

We both laugh just as Steph steps back out onto the deck. She sits down beside me and reaches for my hand.

"Peaches," Tom says softly.

Steph's cheeks flush. "It's my shampoo."

"Reminds me of summers on my granddad's peach farm in Virginia. Have I ever told you about that, Brandon?"

Steph and I share a smile.

"No, Tom, you never have."

"I haven't? Well, I was probably twelve years old . . ."

We spend the rest of the afternoon listening to Staff Sergeant Tom McBride tell us about his summers on his grandfather's farm. I listen to his voice and I commit it to memory, because I never want to forget it.

I never want to forget him.

chapter

twenty-five

Stephanie

"Say it with me."

"Say what?"

" 'My name is Stephanie James, and I am a book hoarder.' "

As I stare at the disaster of books on my bedroom floor, it's really hard to argue with my best friend.

But I do it anyway.

"I am not a hoarder. I just love my books."

Tessa examines the spine of my old paperback copy of Judy Blume's *Forever*. "You know, when I was thirteen, I thought this book was scandalous. I was so innocent back then."

"I used to sit in the back of my high school library and read it." I nod toward the paperback in her hand. "I checked it out so much the librarian finally just gave it to me."

She laughs and adds the book to the box. "Maybe you should have been a librarian instead of an English teacher."

"Maybe. Too late now." With a deep sigh, I take a good look around my bedroom. "You know, I don't remember *un*packing all this stuff. Where did it come from?"

"Hoarder," Tessa whispers, and I throw a pillow at her head.

"Careful now. I'm carrying your niece, you know."

"Xavier says it's my nephew."

"Whatever." She rolls her eyes, but I know she secretly loves it.

It's been two weeks since she told Xavier he was going to be a father, and according to Tessa, his reaction was fairly epic.

She didn't go into detail, but I heard there were tears.

From there, everything just fell into place with their families, basically because the parents didn't have a choice. Xavier immediately adopted a "We're having a baby and we don't give a crap what you think" attitude, which impressed his parents and reassured hers that he was going to take care of their daughter and grandchild.

"So, Mommy, have you thought any more about Xavier's proposal?"

She makes a face. "No, I have not. He hadn't proposed to me *before* we got pregnant. Why should he propose now?"

"Because you're going to be together forever anyway. You might as well get started."

"Well, what about you and Brandon?"

"What about us?"

"What if he proposed before he went off to training? Would you say yes?"

I shake my head and reach for another empty box.

"Brandon and I are in a totally different situation. We've only been together a few months."

"But you want him forever, right?"

"I do, but we realize it's way too soon to be making any sort of commitment to each other. Maybe later, when we have a better idea of where we will be."

"Where *we* will be?"

I throw another pillow at her head.

Smiling sweetly, Tessa stands up and starts removing what few posters and pictures I have hanging around the room.

"It's not like I don't *want* to marry Xavier," she says. "I just don't want the baby to be the reason we do it."

"I know. But he was going to ask eventually."

"But he wouldn't have asked *now*."

I place the lid on the box and stack it with the others next to the door. "I still think you should consider it. And that's the last thing I'll say on the subject."

"Good, because now I have a serious question to ask you."

"Shoot."

"Where are all these boxes going?"

"With me, back to Mom's for the summer."

"And then?"

"And then I don't know."

Tessa pushes another box in my direction, and I add it to the heap.

"You are applying to teach, right?"

"Of course."

She narrows her eyes.

"Okay, I haven't applied anywhere yet. Technically, I can't until I graduate."

"And then you'll apply, right?"

Trying to avoid eye contact, I glance around my bare bedroom. "We've done a good job in here. Ready for the pantry?"

Tessa nods and follows me out of my room toward the kitchen. Truthfully, there isn't much to pack. She took all the fun appliances with her when she moved. I didn't mind. The professional grade mixer and food processor would have just collected dust if she'd left them behind.

She starts in the pantry, tossing out-of-date cans and boxes into the trash while I head to the drawers.

"Does every house have a junk drawer?" I wonder aloud.

"Yes. And you didn't answer my question, Steph."

With a sigh, I leaf through a mound of junk mail before throwing it all in the trash.

"Of course I'll apply somewhere, Tessa."

"Yes, but when?"

"When I know exactly where Brandon will be stationed."

Tessa nods and continues clearing out my cabinet. She doesn't have to say it, but I can feel the disapproval radiating from her. I know what she's thinking, and she's not wrong.

I'm putting my life on hold for Brandon.

"It just seems pointless, Tessa. Why apply for jobs when I don't even know where I'll be?"

An old box of cereal flies through the air, landing in the garbage can.

"And what if you miss out on a really great job opportunity?" she asks.

"There will be other great job opportunities."

"How do you know?"

"I don't *know*, Tessa. I wish I had a crystal ball that would give me all the answers I need, but I don't. For the first time in my life, I'm choosing to have faith. I love him. We are going to make it work, no matter what."

"And that's all wonderful, but what if Brandon is stationed somewhere you can't go? Then you're alone *and* unemployed."

I slam the drawer shut. "Why are you doing this?"

Tessa sighs softly and closes the pantry door. "I just hate to see you put your life on hold. You've worked so hard, Steph. The girl who always has a plan suddenly doesn't have one at all. It makes me nervous for you."

"But we *do* have a plan. Once he gets his post, I'll start applying for teaching jobs in the area. Some of the schools don't start until after Labor Day anyway. If I can't go with him, then I'll stay with Mom and apply to schools in Indianapolis. I'll find something, even if I have to substitute teach for a while."

Defeated and tired, I drop into one of the kitchen chairs.

"Tessa, I can only control so much. I'm trying to stay positive and hopeful, and having you question it really upsets me considering I've done nothing but be supportive of you."

"Steph, I didn't mean—"

"Yes, you did mean it, and I get it. I do. Yes, I'm choosing to put my life on hold for a few months, but I'm doing it in hopes that it will lead to years of something wonderful. Can't you, of all people, understand that?"

Tessa nods and walks toward me. She falls slowly to her knees and takes my hands in hers.

"See, you *do* have a plan. I should have known that you would."

"Yes, you should've." I smile down at her. "Now get off the floor before you make your water break or something."

"I don't think that can happen yet. The baby is the size of a plum."

We laugh and help each other to our feet.

"To thank you for helping me pack, I'm taking you out to lunch."

Her eyes brighten. "Ooh, can we get pancakes?"

"Pancakes? Is this one of those weird pregnancy cravings?"

"Must be. I want pancakes all the time. And baked beans."

I make a face. "I hope not at the same time."

"Had both for dinner last night."

"Gag."

"Don't knock it 'til you try it, Steph."

We laugh and head out the door. As I drive us to the nearest breakfast place, I can't help but wonder if this might be the last lunch we'll have together before graduation. It's just a few weeks away, and between finals and packing, neither of us have a lot of free time. Once we have our degrees, Tessa will be headed to Chicago with Xavier and I'll be . . . well, I don't know where I'll be. Normally that would scare the crap out of me, but all I feel is hopeful.

Good things are coming, and for the first time in my life, I'm excited that I have absolutely no idea what that means. Maybe that's because I know that, regardless of where I am, I'll still be his, and Brandon will still be mine.

That knowledge makes me brave.

Brave enough to try baked beans with my pancakes, much to my best friend's absolute delight.

Later that evening, I call Mom to give her the date and time of our graduation. She and Brandon talk for a few minutes before telling each other goodnight. After handing me the phone, he kisses my forehead and then calls for Bangle. The cat leaps out of my lap and follows him down the hallway.

"You know, out of all the surprises this semester, I have to say my cat's growing affection for Brandon has to be the most unexpected of all."

"Getting close are they?"

"They cuddle now."

Mom laughs. "I can't believe it's only a week until graduation. You're all packed?"

"Pretty much. Everything that can be packed is boxed up and ready to go." I cradle the phone close to my ear and take a deep breath. "I . . . kinda wanted to talk to you about where to store them."

"I assumed you'd bring them home."

"You did?"

"Of course."

I breathe a sigh of relief.

"Are you coming home with them?"

"I actually wanted to talk to you about that, too"

So I tell her about my plan to live with her throughout the summer, and to hold off on applying for a job until I know the location of Brandon's post.

"And if you can't go with him?" she asks.

"Then I'll apply for jobs in and around Indianapolis. And I'll find my own apartment."

She laughs. "Steph, you're welcome to live with me for as long as you want. You know I miss having you around."

"But?"

"Well, I am a little concerned about you putting your life on hold."

"You did it for Dad."

The words are out before I can stop them, but I wouldn't take them back even if I could. After my conversation with Tessa this afternoon, I expected the same from my mom.

"You're right, I did."

"Do you regret that decision?"

"No, because it gave me you."

I fumble with the chain around my neck. I've stopped hiding it beneath my clothes. It's always visible now, and always around my neck. I only take it off to sleep. I'm too afraid it'll become tangled and break.

"Mom, I don't see this as me putting my life on hold. I'm just waiting a few months. Once we find out where he'll be on a permanent basis, then I'll decide what to do."

She grows silent, which is unusual for my mom. She's never been shy about voicing her disapproval.

"Mom, do you remember at the beginning of this semester when you asked me to do something adventurous before I devote the rest of my life to my teaching career?"

"Vaguely," she mutters, but I know better. Mom never forgets a thing.

"I love him, Mom."

"I know you do."

"Just the fact that I am in love is an adventure. The fact that I'm in love with a soldier is the ultimate adventure."

"No, that's a miracle."

We both laugh.

"Mom, we want to be together. I hope I can go with him. We can't live together, but we could at least be in the same town. If I can't, I'll cross that bridge when I get there, but for now, I am trying to have faith. I'm placing my hopes in the hands of the military gods that he gets a good post. For me, that's about as adventurous as it gets."

Mom chuckles softly. "I must say, it sounds like you have it all planned out."

"I have it as planned out as I can. I'll deal with the rest when it comes."

After we hang up, I turn off the lights and head to our bedroom. Brandon's fast asleep, with Bangle curled around his feet. I change out of my clothes and slip on one of his shirts . . . a khaki tee, with *Army Strong* printed across the chest. I slip my dad's ID tags over my head and place them gently on top of the dresser.

With the light spilling in through the curtains, I'm able to catch my reflection in the dresser mirror. I gaze thoughtfully at the girl in the glass. On the outside, she's not really all that different from the girl she was at the beginning of the semester. Her hair's a little longer and she's lost a few pounds, but other than that, she's the same girl.

On the outside.

But on the inside, there has been a seismic shift. In her attitude, her personality, and in her faith. She's let go of the bitter chain she carried for far too long, allowing her to open her eyes and her heart to the type of man she never imagined she could love, but now, can't imagine living without.

Stephanie James has finally grown up.

As I climb into bed and snuggle deep into Brandon's arms, I can't help but think that's what college is really all about. It's not just a bunch of classes and parties. It's not just sports and lectures. It's about finding the person you're meant to be.

And if you're lucky, the person you're meant to be with.

chapter
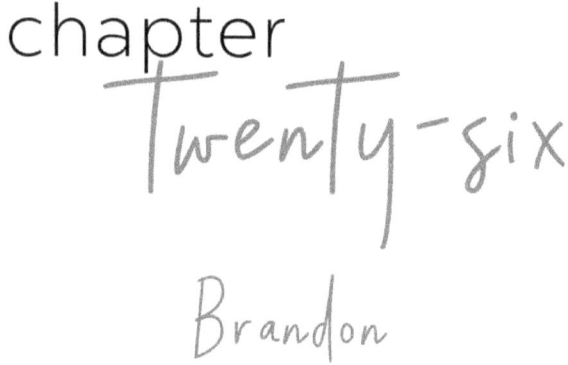

Twenty-six

Brandon

Graduation.

Some people never have one.

A few of my friends back in Applewood dropped out before graduating high school. Of those who did make it, most of them didn't go on to college. A lot of them started working in the mines, which is one of the hardest jobs in the world. Some found minimum wage jobs in our little town, or moved to nearby places like Pikeville or Hazard, hoping to find work. Other friends disappeared completely, and I haven't seen them since walking across the stage of Applewood High.

As I prepare for my second graduation of the day—my ROTC Commissioning Ceremony—I can't help but think about my mother. In just a few minutes, I will no longer be a cadet. I will be commissioned as a second lieutenant in the United States Army, and she's not here to see it.

Would she be proud? I have no idea.

I've spent so much time *not* thinking about her that it surprises me that today would be the day I'd feel her absence the most. She's missing so much. She didn't see me receiving my bachelor's degree this morning. She missed watching the woman I love receive hers. And she'll never meet her beautiful granddaughters.

I fasten the last button on my uniform and look at myself in the full-length mirror.

It's time to stop wasting time and energy feeling sorry for the choice she made.

I join my fellow cadets, and we shake each other's hands before forming a line and entering the small auditorium. Six of us are being commissioned today. This graduation is low-key but still formal, with about fifty guests sitting in the audience. Behind them, the remaining cadets sit in their Class A uniforms.

As the colonel welcomes everyone to the ceremony, I scan the room in search of my family. Christian and the girls are in the third row, and sitting next to them is my father, smiling proudly in his uniform. Dr. Edsall reminded us it was a risk, him making the five-hour trip to Indiana just for a pinning ceremony, but I wanted him here, and in his most lucid moments, he *wanted* to be here. If all goes well, he'll have a very important role today.

So far, so good.

Tessa and Xavier are here, too. They both graduated this morning—she with her degree in

Culinary Arts and Xavier with his in Sports Management. Tomorrow, they're off to Chicago, but they wanted to stay for my ROTC ceremony. They've become two of my best friends, and they constantly remind me that blood doesn't make you family.

And of course there's Steph, in a black dress and a pair of killer heels that make me wonder why she doesn't wear heels more often. She's sitting next to my dad, holding his hand. Cynthia, her mom, is right by her side.

Another reminder that blood doesn't make you family.

The colonel asks us to stand and raise our right hand. One by one, we repeat after him, taking our oath of office as appointed second lieutenants in the United States Army.

"Cadet Walker will now be pinned by his father, Major General Bruce Walker, and his sister, Ms. Christian Young."

I stand stock still while my sister helps Dad to the front of the stage. Stepping forward, I smile at them as the colonel begins to speak once again.

"Brandon Lee Walker graduates today as both a distinguished military graduate and Magna Cum Laude with a Bachelor of Science degree in Computer Engineering. He is receiving the United States Army commission of second lieutenant and will attend Signal Corps Training at Fort Gordon this summer."

While the colonel tells the audience my future goals, during and after my military service, my dad, steady and strong, pins my insignia to each of my shoulders. He takes a step back, his eyes ghosting over my uniform while my sister hugs me. When she steps away, I look to my father once again and wonder if he even knows where he is. If he recognizes me. If he understands the significance of this moment—to him and to me.

Suddenly, his face turns stoic and his body is ramrod straight as he lifts his hand to his brow.

And then he salutes me.

My eyes swim with tears as I lift my hand to salute my father.

There's applause, but it's all white noise, because my dad steps closer to me. With his eyes shining with clarity, he smiles before wrapping his arms around me, hugging me tightly.

"I'm proud of you, Brandon," he whispers, his voice full of emotion.

In that moment, I know he *is* here . . . alert and aware. Proud and happy. And he just hugged me. I can't remember the last time my dad hugged me.

And that makes today one of the best days of my life.

chapter
Twenty-seven
Stephanie

Today is one of the worst days of my life.

Mom says I'm being melodramatic. It's just twelve weeks. It's not like he's going to Iraq. Or Afghanistan. Or some other war-torn country where people are just waiting to shoot at him.

He's going to Georgia. What could possibly happen to him in *Georgia*?

With a sigh, I toss a pebble into the pond and watch it ripple with the breeze. I love this pond. I love the mountains. And I'm pretty sure there's nothing prettier than a Kentucky sunrise. This morning I watched, fascinated, as the sky turned from blood-red to orange, with swirls of pink and blue brushed across the horizon's edge.

Will a Georgia sunrise be just as pretty?

I can't imagine it.

Of course, I can't imagine a lot of things. Like how Brandon's two-week leave ends today. Or, how tomorrow night, he'll be sleeping at Fort Gordon, and I'll be back home in Indiana.

Last week, Brandon and I had moved all my belongings, including my cat, back to Mom's house. We didn't stay long, mainly because I wanted Brandon to spend as much time with his family as possible. Selfishly, and because neither of us can stand to be away from the other for more than a day, I followed him home to Applewood.

It hasn't really been a relaxing time for anyone.

Mr. Walker has had some rough nights, which means the rest of us have, too. Even though the trip to graduation was a definite success, he just hasn't been the same since his return home. His bad days outnumber his good, and I can't help but wonder what kind of father will be waiting for Brandon when he gets back from AIT.

A lot can happen in twelve weeks.

"There you are."

I look over my shoulder to find Brandon walking onto the dock.

"How was your run?"

He sits down beside me. "It was good. Why are you up so early?"

"I love the Kentucky sunrise. I'm going to miss it."

"I'll miss it, too."

"I was just wondering if a Georgia sunrise would be just as pretty."

"I don't see how."

I smile. "And the bed was cold."

"Steph, it's summer."

"The bed was still cold."

He grins and leans over, kissing me on the cheek.

"I guess I need to get used to it, huh? Cold beds, I mean."

Brandon dips his head and kisses my shoulder. "I'm afraid so. For the next twelve weeks, anyway."

"And after that?"

I shouldn't ask, because I know the answer. After that, if I want a warm bed, we'll have to get married. The United States Army won't let us live in sin.

"After that is up to you, Steph."

"What does that mean?"

Brandon sighs and looks out across the water. "It just means I'm going to miss you. And when I get back, I'm going to want you in my bed all the time."

"But you have to live in the barracks."

"Yep. Unless . . ."

Unless we get married.

"Breakfast is ready!" Christian yells from the porch.

Brandon sighs and takes my hand, helping me to my feet. He doesn't say it, but I know what he's thinking.

It's his last day home, and he wants it to be a good one.

I don't pray a lot, but as we walk hand in hand toward the house, I find myself doing just that.

Please let Mr. Walker have a good day. Please let Brandon have a proper goodbye with his dad. And please don't let me spoil it with my tears.

Brandon spends the afternoon rolling around on the floor with his nieces and having quiet talks with his dad. He also makes sure that Christian can use the video chat program on her laptop so they can talk while he's at AIT. For dinner, Christian and I make Brandon's favorite meal—fried chicken and mashed potatoes. Once dinner is over and the dishes are cleared, Christian helps Mr. Walker to bed while Uncle Brandon reads a bedtime story to the girls.

This gives me the chance to do what I've wanted to do all day.

I walk up to Brandon's bedroom, close the door, sit down on his bed, and cry like a baby.

Because it's hit me. It really hits me that he's going to be gone for three months. After that, he will be gone for even longer, and there's a chance I won't be able to go with him.

What if I can't go? What if I only see him a few weeks each year? Can we handle that? Can our relationship survive that?

I don't even know he's in the room until I feel him kneel at my feet.

"Hey," he whispers. "What is this?"

I wipe my eyes. "This is me being a baby, and I'm sorry. I've tried to be tough. I have tried to hold it in, but it finally just hit me. I'm sorry that I can't be strong like you."

He takes my hands in his. "I'm not strong, Steph. I just keep telling myself it's twelve weeks. Three months and I'll be back. I'll get a few weeks leave, maybe even a whole month, before I have to report to my post. And I pray it's close to home, Steph. I pray it's close to you. So I'm not strong. I'm just doing what you told me to do."

"What did I tell you to do?"

"You told me to have faith. You said that we will make it work, no matter what."

I nod. "I did say that."

"Yes, you did." He gently wipes my tears away with his fingertips. "And after AIT, and once we know where my post will be, you and I need to have a serious conversation about the future."

My teary eyes widen. "Didn't we already have one of those?"

"We did, but I think it's time to have another one. I love you, Steph. And if Dad's disease is teaching me anything, it's that you have to choose to be happy, because one day your body, or your mind, may take that choice away from. I love you. I'm never going to love anybody else. My family loves you. And I want you in my life, no matter where I am. No matter what it takes."

Fresh tears trickle down my cheek.

"Brandon Walker, don't you dare propose to me. Not now. Not right before you leave."

"Okay."

I frown.

He smirks.

"*Okay*?"

"Okay. You told me not to propose to you, so I won't."

"But you were going to?"

He shrugs. "I thought about it."

Seriously? "But I thought . . . I thought you said we weren't ready."

Brandon kisses my tear-stained cheeks before pushing me back against the mattress and crawling up my body. We kiss, his mouth moving against my lips and along my skin with a frantic urgency, as if he's memorizing every inch of me.

"Maybe we aren't ready to get married tonight," Brandon murmurs against my throat. "But I know one thing for certain."

"What's that?"

His eyes find mine in the darkness, and he smiles.

"I bet we'll be ready in twelve weeks," he whispers.

chapter

Twenty-eight

Stephanie

"Don't you think it's time you joined the rest of the world?"

I place my bookmark against the page before looking up at my mom.

"I'm outside. What more do you want?"

She sits down beside me. "Well, I'd like for you to take a shower, get dressed, and do something today besides sit on this porch and read books that make you cry."

I don't tell her it's not the books that make me cry. They're just a convenient and plausible excuse.

"It's been six weeks, Steph. You're halfway there."

"I'm aware of the calendar. Trust me."

"Remember what Brandon said on the phone last night?"

I sigh.

"He will be very disappointed if I don't do something fun this summer. He doesn't want me to sit around being all depressed."

"Exactly."

"So we won't tell him."

Mom smiles.

"I must say, you do seem to be sleeping better."

Not really. My body had finally just surrendered to exhaustion. The first few weeks after Brandon left had been torture, especially at night. I'd gotten too accustomed to having him beside me.

"The bed was too cold," I whisper.

She doesn't ask what that means. I think if anyone can understand the concept of an empty bed, it's my mom.

"I don't know how you do it, Mom. And I don't know how you've done it for the past twenty-two years."

Mom takes my hand. "I had you to help keep my bed warm."

"So what you're saying is I need a kid."

Her eyes grow wide.

"Relax. I'm kidding."

She sighs heavily and pushes off with her feet, making the porch swing sway in the summer breeze.

"I was thinking that you and I should maybe have a talk about that," Mom says.

"A talk about what?"

"Kids."

I'm not stupid. She doesn't want to talk about kids. She wants to talk about sex, and she wants to know if I'm having it. While my brain screams that

I'm twenty-two years old and it's really none of her business, I can't ignore the fact that this is my mom, and we've never had any secrets.

"No worries, Mom. I'm still the virginal daughter I've always been."

Virginal, but not entirely innocent.

I can tell by the expression on her face she doesn't believe me. It hurts a little, but then I consider the fact that Brandon and I are adults and have been roommates for nearly four months. Of course she assumes.

"Seriously, Mom. Brandon and I talked about it. No matter how much we were tempted, we decided to wait. Then Tessa got pregnant and I was *so* relieved we waited. Until we know for sure where he'll be and that we can be together, I'm just too afraid to chance it. Plus, I can't imagine . . . being that close and then having to say goodbye."

"It's torture," Mom whispers.

Tears fill my eyes.

She clears her throat. "I'm very glad to hear that you're waiting, Stephanie, because I would hate . . ."

"You'd hate what?"

"I would hate for history to repeat itself."

I frown.

"Stephanie, I haven't been entirely honest with you about something, and I'm only doing it now because I want you to keep it in mind when Brandon returns from leave. When he comes home, the two of you are going to want to . . . be close. And I know you say that you want to be responsible and wait until you're sure you can be together on a permanent basis, but take it from someone who knows. Hormones take over. Love takes over. And any thought of being noble and responsible just . . . disappears."

I give her hand a reassuring squeeze. She bows her head and takes a deep breath.

"Your father and I loved each other very much. That was never a question. But he wasn't eager to get married right after high school. Not as eager as I was, anyway. He had already proposed. I had a ring on my finger. But he was perfectly content to have a long engagement. At that time, he wanted to be a soldier more than he wanted to be a husband."

"What changed his mind?"

Mom eyes swim with tears.

"You did."

I blink. *What?*

"The only reason the two of you got married was because you were pregnant with me?"

"The reason we got married before he went to Basic was because I was pregnant, yes."

I narrow my eyes. "But you always told me you found out you were pregnant while he was gone to Basic."

"That's what I told you, yes. That's what we told everyone."

"Why did you lie?"

"We were afraid of disappointing our parents—
"

"No. Why did you lie to me?"

She sighs. "Because you are my daughter, and you already carried enough grief on your shoulders. I know you, Stephanie. If I had told you the truth, you would've always wondered if the only reason your father and I got married was because I was pregnant with you. And you would somehow twist that into believing that it's your fault I'm alone."

"But it *is* my fault you're alone. If I hadn't come along, you would have married someone else."

"See, I knew you'd make that leap."

"It's not a leap. It's the truth." I shake my head in amazement. "Anyway, why are you telling me this now? Why would you keep this from me all my life and choose to tell me now?"

"Because I see the way you and Brandon look at each other. I watch his eyes glaze over whenever you walk into a room. And I've heard you cry yourself to sleep for the past six weeks. I just want you to be prepared for the rollercoaster of emotions you're going to feel when he comes home."

The phone rings, and Mom leans over to kiss the top of my head before walking back into the house.

I wish I could say the remaining six weeks are a blur, but every single second crawls along like an inchworm. At Brandon's insistence, I apply for teaching positions at a few of the junior high and high schools in and around Indianapolis. The chances of him being stationed in Indiana are slim, so I'm not at all heartbroken when my resumes and applications go unnoticed by the local school boards.

During our last call, Brandon told me that some of the soldiers had received news about their first post. Some are staying at Fort Gordon. Others are headed overseas. A buddy of Brandon's from Montana is being sent to Fort Knox, Kentucky.

If only we could get so lucky.

While we wait for news, I glue myself to my laptop, learning everything I can about Army bases, particularly the ones with schools. I make a list of job opportunities at some of the regional bases, like Fort Knox, Fort Campbell, and where Brandon's currently training, Fort Gordon. I check real estate in the areas, and then, just to have all the information, I spend some time learning everything I can about actually living on base.

One night, I even find an online chat devoted to Army wives.

I create an account. I don't want to lie, so I don't introduce myself. I tell them I'm just there to listen. So that's what I do. I listen to their stories, and I'm blown away by the sacrifices they make each and every day. Despite the struggles, and there are many, these women still talk about their husbands with such love and pride.

I'm lying across my bed, with Bangle by my side. I've just logged in to the group when my video chat screen pops up.

Incoming call from Brandon.

Feeling giddy, I quickly log out and accept the call. The screen flickers to life, and then he's there, smiling at me with his dimples and camo cap.

"Hey, babe."

He's started calling me *babe*. It's the cutest thing ever.

"Hey."

"Why aren't you sleeping?"

"I could ask you the same question."

He shrugs. "Couldn't sleep. Too excited. I was going to send you a text, but then I saw that you were online. You okay?"

"I'm okay. Are you okay?"

"I'm fantastic."

"Fantastic?"

"Couldn't be happier. Well, I *could* be . . ."

I grin.

"What's made you so happy?"

"I have news."

My mouth goes dry.

"Good news?"

He nods. "I think so. Remember our last day at my dad's? When you asked if a Georgia sunrise could be as pretty as a Kentucky dawn?"

"Yeah . . ."

"You're gonna get the chance to find out."

With those words, I burst into tears. I can't talk for crying. So I just cry and cry, because I know we're going to be together. He wouldn't be this happy if we couldn't be.

"After AIT graduation, my post will be here at Fort Gordon. I'll be developing and implementing upgrades to the communications and security systems here on base."

I smile at the screen. "I don't even know what that means."

Brandon laughs. "It's okay. You don't have to know what it means."

"For how long?"

"Eighteen months," he says. "It's just six hours from home, which isn't bad at all. I have to live on base, but we knew that."

Because he's single.

"Yeah."

"But I've been looking around. There are plenty of apartment complexes close by. There are three school systems. There's even a school on base, and the teachers are mostly civilians. Can you teach in Georgia? I don't know how that works. I guess you'd need to get certified. . ." His voice trails off when he notices I'm not saying a word. "Babe?"

"I'm here."

He grins and places his hand on the screen. I do the same. We know it's cheesy, but it's ridiculously comforting.

"You're not *here*. Not yet. But I want you to be . . . if you want to be."

"I want to be."

We smile stupidly at each other.

"Almost over, babe. I'll be home in two weeks."

It's late, and he has an early morning PT, so we make plans to talk to each other tomorrow night.

"I love you, Steph."

"I love you, too."

He gives me a wink, and then the screen disappears.

The next two weeks *are* a blur because I don't stop. The very next morning, I begin making lists and formulating a plan. I get online and learn all I can about Fort Gordon, Georgia. I scope out apartments, schools, restaurants, and libraries. After contacting the state's education department, I learn that I will need to take another test in order to be certified to teach in Georgia. After registering for that, I then turn my attention to searching for a place to live. Finding one in my price range is difficult. Finding one that allows pets is even harder.

Overwhelmed, I call my pregnant best friend for support.

"I don't understand," she says. "Why can't you live on base?"

"Because we aren't married."

"Okay. And why does he *have* to live on base?"

"Because we aren't married."

"Hmm. This sound like an easy problem to solve."

My ear's going numb, so I put her on speakerphone.

"Not really. Even if we were married, we'd probably be wait-listed for military housing. We could get an apartment off base, though."

"So you've thought about it."

"Sure, I've thought about it. You know me. I have to consider all options."

"I do know you. It sounds like a lot of this would be solved if *someone* would propose. Need me to make a call? Because if I know soldier boy, he is dying to ask you to marry him. I bet I could have you engaged by lunch time."

I laugh. "No, Tessa. I don't want to get married just because of the housing allowance."

"Well, there are other benefits, too. Like insurance."

"Tessa!"

"I'm serious. You don't realize how important insurance is until you're pregnant and don't have any."

Mom chooses that moment to walk through the kitchen. She stops, raises an eyebrow, and then nods in agreement.

"Tessa was just describing all the perks of being an Army wife."

"I see."

"Am I on speaker?" Tessa whispers, which is hilarious. Even if you're whispering on speaker, you're still *on speaker*.

Mom steps closer to the phone. "Hello, Tessa. How are you feeling, sweetheart?"

"Oh, hi Cynthia! Ugh, I'm so fat. My feet are swollen. My *boobs* are swollen. And we can't decide on a baby name."

I don't tell her it would probably be easier to settle on a name if they knew the sex. But she and Xavier are adamant about keeping the baby's gender a mystery.

After we hang up, I take my laptop and head out to the porch swing. Mom is there, reading today's newspaper.

I sit down beside her and look toward the sky.

"Rain's coming."

She nods. "We're due a thunderstorm. It's been a day or so."

I nod and open my laptop.

"Stephanie, I can't deny I'm a little hurt. If you wanted to discuss the perks of being an Army wife, I would have thought you'd come to me."

My fingers freeze on the keyboard. "Oh, Mom, that was Tessa just being silly."

"Was it? I can't imagine as close as you and Brandon are that the conversation hasn't come up at least once."

"Twice."

She smiles.

"It *would* solve the apartment issue, Steph."

"Like that's a reason to get married."

"So what is a reason to get married?"

"Are we seriously having this conversation?"

"I think we should. What is a reason to get married?"

I sigh heavily and close my laptop.

"Because you love each other."

"Yes."

"Because you never want to be without him."

"Keep going."

"Because . . . you can't imagine growing old and gray with anyone but him. Because he loves your cat. And your obsession with the 80s. And he has dimples and a kickass Inigo Montoya T-shirt."

"Inigo . . . what?"

"And he loves me, Mom. He really loves me."

"I know, sweetheart."

I don't realize I'm crying until she hands me a tissue.

"Love like that is rare," she says softly. "Personally? I wouldn't waste a second of it."

"You *didn't* waste a second of it. That's why you got married so young."

Mom smiles.

"You're right. I didn't waste a second of it. And you shouldn't either."

chapter

Twenty-nine

Brandon

Pale Kentucky moonlight streams through my windshield. Stifling a yawn, I crank up the radio, hoping the music will keep me awake.

Just a few miles to go, Brandon.

It's been a long day. Up at four thirty for my final PT and breakfast with my unit and then hours of out-processing leading up to AIT graduation. My certificates lay in the seat beside me, ready to be framed.

Christian had already told me that Dr. Edsall didn't approve of another long trip for Dad, so I let everyone off the hook and told them to skip this graduation. I didn't mind. It was a short ceremony, and I planned to head home immediately after anyway. I think Christian was secretly relieved. Steph, however, took some convincing, so we compromised.

I told her she could be waiting for me tonight.

In my bed. Where she belongs.

With that thought in mind, I press my foot a little harder against the gas.

A gentle rain begins to fall as I pull into the driveway. After grabbing my gear out of the cab, I walk quietly into the house, hoping Duke is fast asleep somewhere. I hope everyone's asleep. It's past midnight, and I don't need a welcoming committee. I'm content with seeing them all in the morning.

Well, almost all of them.

After taking a quick peek in on Dad to make sure he's sleeping okay, I head up to my room. It's absolutely ridiculous that I'm nervous, but I am. Twelve weeks isn't an eternity, but it's a long time to go without kissing the woman you love.

If I have it my way, after tonight, I'll be able to kiss her anytime I want.

Taking a deep breath, I open the door and step inside the room. It's dark, so it takes a moment for my eyes to adjust. Then they do, and I see her lying on my bed, wrapped in my blanket. Her eyes are closed, and I can hear her quiet snores.

Carefully, I place my gear on the floor and sit down at my desk to unlace my boots. I should probably shower, but I'm too excited and too anxious to hold her in my arms.

As I climb into bed, a bolt of lightning flashes in the window, illuminating her face. Her brown hair is longer now, and it fans out across the pillow.

I want to watch her sleep. I want to kiss her awake.

Suddenly, thunder rumbles overhead, and my choice is made for me.

Steph's eyes flash open.

"Hey, you."

She blinks a few times before her face breaks out into the most beautiful grin I've ever seen. With a sweet laugh, she grabs me, pulling me down on top of her.

For the first few minutes, all we do is stare at each other. Maybe because we can. Or maybe because we're looking for little things we might have missed while we were apart.

"Your hair's longer," I whisper.

"Yours is shorter. I didn't think that was possible."

She sighs softly, her eyes flickering to my mouth.

"So, Lieutenant Walker, are you gonna kiss me or not?"

"I'm thinking about it."

"You think too much."

She rolls us over, and we both groan as she covers her body with mine. Steph kisses me, and from the very second her lips touch mine, with all their frantic urgency and sweet warmth, I know in my heart that something has changed. Our kisses have changed. Our touch has changed. *We've* changed. There's a craving there. A deep and powerful yearning that wasn't there before and can only come from spending time apart. It makes us kiss one another a little slower, hold each other a little tighter, and love each other a little more than we did just twelve weeks ago.

Steph suddenly lifts herself up, straddling my waist and sliding her hands along my stomach. Another flash of lightning in the sky shows me what she's wearing.

It's my *Princess Bride* T-shirt, the same one I was wearing the day we met in class.

"Nice shirt."

"Thanks. I stole it from your closet before you left. I've slept in it every night."

"Thief."

With a sly grin, she leans down and kisses me again.

"You've stolen my clothes. Stolen my heart."

Steph smiles against my lips.

"There's something else I want to steal," she whispers.

I slide my hands along her back, pulling her closer to me as I raise myself up. Wrapping her arms around my neck, she melts against me when I bury my face against her neck.

"I'll give you anything, Steph."

"Anything?"

"Whatever you want."

I lift my head and find her eyes, deep and dark and full of tears. All of her earlier playfulness is gone as she places her palm against my cheek.

"I want your last name."

My mouth falls open, but words fail me.

"Before you say yes or no, I want to tell you all the reasons why I want your last name. I made a list."

"You made a list?"

"Of course, I make a list for everything. But this list is not on paper. It's . . . in my head. And in my heart."

She made a list. She wants my last name.

"I've thought about it a lot over the past three months," she says softly. "I love you, Brandon. You love me, and you loved me even when I was pretty unlovable. I was judgmental and bitter and way too focused on the future instead of living for today. You love my cat, and my cat loves you, which is a miracle because until you came along, she didn't love anybody but me. You and your family have taught me that life is short, and you have to find joy whenever and wherever you can. I missed you. I don't think I realized until I woke up and saw you there just how much I missed you. And I don't want to miss you anymore."

I pull her close. "Babe—"

Fresh tears spill down her cheeks. "And I know there may come a time when you're stationed somewhere I can't be, but if I *can* be . . . that's where I want to be. And I don't want to live in an apartment by myself while you sleep in the barracks. I want to be *with* you. In your arms. In your bed. Right where I belong."

She finally takes a breath, and I kiss the corners of her mouth.

"Stephanie James, are you proposing to me?"

"That depends."

"On?"

"Are you saying yes?"

I smile into her shining eyes. I don't tell her she's ruined my surprise. I don't mention that I already called her mom, asking for her blessing. And I definitely don't tell her about the ring that's in my bag.

Instead, I cradle her beautiful face in my hands and whisper one word.

"Yes."

epilogue

Stephanie

Six Months Later

Sundays are my favorite day of the week. No five o'clock workouts. No papers to grade. No projects to design or lesson plans to create. It's the one day of the week we can spend together without interruption, giving us the chance to work on this newlywed thing.

We're getting pretty good at it.

Wrapping my arms around his neck, I straddle his waist as he lifts himself, brushing his chest against my bare skin. The sensation sends a spike of tingles up my spine, causing my body to bow. Brandon quickens his pace and tightens his hold on my bottom, anchoring me to his body. He whispers my name against my throat, and my eyes flutter closed because every single touch is electric against my flesh.

Will it always be like this?

It wasn't, not in the beginning. Our wedding night wasn't like this. I was inexperienced and clueless. He was nervous and needy. I'd *begged* him to let us practice before the honeymoon, but I was a virgin, and he was determined to keep me that way until our wedding night.

Needless to say, it was a short engagement.

A week, to be exact.

Despite our mutual fumbling, we figured it out pretty quickly. Once that ring was on my finger, Brandon was all about practicing. Thanks to our practice sessions, I know how much my husband loves it when I rake my fingernails down his back. And he's learned that he can make my entire body tremble just by sliding his tongue along the column of my throat.

We practice a lot.

Suddenly, he scrapes his teeth across my skin. My entire body convulses, and I shatter into a million pieces. Brandon groans, burying his face against my neck and holding me tight as he falls over the edge with me.

Oh, how I love Sundays.

I collapse against him, breathless and exhausted, while Brandon pulls the blanket around us. We must disturb the cat, because she chooses that moment to finally jump down from the bed.

"Oh, *now* you move," Brandon mutters.

Bangle meows loudly in response and trots out of the bedroom.

I laugh and snuggle against his chest. "She does it on purpose."

"That's a sick cat you have, Mrs. Walker."

"What's mine is ours, Lieutenant Walker."

Ours.

It's a beautiful word, filled with the promise that no matter what happens, he is mine. And I'm his.

And this is our house.

It's small, with two bedrooms and a garage, but there's a big backyard for Duke. Base housing wasn't available, and the wait list was ridiculous, so we found a place to rent off base that's close to Fort Gordon and a short commute to my school. For now, I'm teaching eighth grade English at one of the local junior highs while the teacher is on maternity leave. I'm hoping this job will lead to a permanent one in the school system next year.

Brandon enjoys his work at the base. He tries to explain his designs and upgrades, but it's all over my head. Right now, he's working on an automated entry system that will improve security on base. The best part is that Brandon gets to come home to me every night, and I get to cook breakfast for my husband each morning.

I'm getting better in the kitchen. Tessa sent a bunch of bakeware and cookbooks as a wedding gift. She and Xavier, and our gorgeous nephew Alexander, are still living in Chicago. Xavier finally convinced her to marry him, and they have an apartment in the city close to her aunt's restaurant.

Tessa's working there as an apprentice chef and Xavier is an assistant basketball coach at one of the high schools.

As for the rest of our family, my mom is still living in Indianapolis but threatens to move to Georgia every day. I'm pretty sure the only thing keeping her in the Hoosier state is her new boyfriend, an attorney named Alan. I've only met him once, and I don't really know how serious they are, but for the first time in twenty-three years, my mom isn't lonely. When we're on the phone, she talks about him constantly. I can tell she's happy, and that's all that matters to me.

One week after I proposed, Brandon and I were married on the dock of his family's pond. It was just a small ceremony, with his family and my mom. There were no bridesmaids or big poofy dresses. Just me in a white sundress, with my dad's dog tags around my neck, and Brandon in his Class A uniform.

Lord, I love his uniform.

Our wedding day was beautiful and bittersweet. We didn't know it at the time, but that day would be the last we'd spend with Mr. Walker in the comfort of his home. Brandon's dad now lives in an assisted-living facility in the nearby city of Pikeville. He will remain there for the rest of his life. It was a hard decision, filled with a lot of guilt and plenty of tears, but his condition had finally declined to the point that Christian just couldn't take care of him on her own. Now, Mr. Walker truly has twenty-four hour care. Our last visit was especially heartbreaking because he didn't recognize any of us. Dr. Edsall had warned us it would happen eventually, but Brandon still took it especially hard. The next day, I drove us back to Georgia, and Brandon didn't say a word all the way home. It's hard, but knowing Mr. Walker has the care he needs, and that Christian can rest a little easier at night, assures all of us that we made the right decision.

Being an Army wife has definitely been a life-changing experience. There's really no other way to describe it. I'm still learning my way around base. Brandon and I shop at the commissary and check out books from the base library. Brandon's made some friends, and luckily for me, they have sweet wives who have welcomed me with open arms.

And now, I can log in to the Army wives online chat without feeling like a phony, and I can tell them I'm the proud wife of a soldier.

Over the past six months, I've learned that, beneath my husband's *Army Strong* exterior, there is a man who loves everything with his whole heart. The military. Our friends. His family. My mom. Even my cat.

And me. Especially me.

Always me.

"Babe?"

"Hmm."

"You're quiet."

I kiss his chest. "Just thinking."

"Good thoughts?"

"The best thoughts."

"Must've been thinking about me, then."

I laugh. And then sometimes, he's not a soldier at all. He's just my Brandon, with his cute dimples and his *Princess Bride* T-shirt, making me laugh and loving me more than I deserve.

Every day is an adventure. Every night is bliss. And I know it can all change in the blink of an eye. Not just because he's in the military, but because that's life. I know we'll struggle at times. Every family has some sort of battle, and we won't be immune to that. We'll soldier on, because that's what we do. But we'll also have joy. We *already* have joy. That joy is even sweeter because I have Brandon by my side.

And to think I could have missed it all, just because he's a soldier.

Growing up, I sometimes thought about my future husband. My very own Prince Charming who would somehow make all my sadness disappear.

I never imagined my prince would wear camouflage.

I never thought I would love a soldier. I never thought I *could*.

Until a soldier loved me.

about the author

USA Today Bestselling Author Sydney Logan writes heartfelt stories that feature strong women and the men who love them. In addition to her novels, she has penned several short stories and is a contributor to Chicken Soup for the Soul. She is a Netflix junkie, music lover, and a Vol for Life. Sydney and her husband make their home in beautiful East Tennessee.

To learn more about Sydney and her books, visit her online at sydneylogan.com.

acknowledgments

I know every author says this, but I truly have the best readers ever. Believe me when I say your reviews are my favorites.

I hope every author has the kind of relationship I have with my editor, Wendy Depperschmidt. Thank you for your dedication to my books and for wanting nothing but the best for me.

Thank you to Kathie Spitz and Shaina Hanson, both of whom read early drafts of this story and then offered to proofread the final product. You've both been with me from the very beginning, and I can't thank you enough!

Thanks to T.M. Franklin for another amazing cover.

JA Hensley is my swag maker, hand holder, cheerleader—the list is endless. I couldn't do it without you!

Special thanks to Kelsey Williams, one of my faithful readers and a military wife. Writing this book took months of ROTC research, and while Kelsey is a proud Navy wife, she found the answers

I needed that hopefully make this story as realistic as possible.

I have to mention Jaime Edsall, who I surprised by using her last name in this book. She's awesome because she sends me Oklahoma wine and shares my books with her Granny, which is the sweetest thing ever. Give CJ a hug for me.

Special thanks to the following people for your support and contributions to this book: Jim & Terri Gislason, Maria Bruce, John Beaty, Heather Lowe, Mackensey Lowe, Tara Phillips, Dakota Phillips, Evie Thomas, Brittney Brown, Angie Ellis, Cynthia Ogg, & Michele Macleod.

Book bloggers are instrumental in getting books into the hands of readers. I would be too afraid to list them because I'd surely leave someone out, but I am so appreciative of the bloggers who help promote my books.

And finally, to my husband, who shares my love for *The Princess Bride* and Inigo Montoya. Thank you for being everything I ever wanted. As you wish.

www.ingramcontent.com/pod-product-compliance
Lightning Source LLC
Chambersburg PA
CBHW051410170626
46809CB00006B/2099